I0823560

OUR PRECIOUS WARS

Perrine Tripier

OUR PRECIOUS WARS

Translated from the French
by Alison Anderson

Europa Editions
27 Union Square West, Suite 302
New York NY 10003
www.europaeditions.com
info@europaeditions.com

This book is a work of fiction. Any references to historical events, real people, or real locales are used fictitiously.

Copyright © Éditions Gallimard, Paris, 2023
First publication 2025 by Europa Editions

Translation by Alison Anderson
Original title: *Les Guerres précieuses*
Translation copyright © 2025 by Europa Editions

All rights reserved, including the right of reproduction in whole or in part in any form.

Library of Congress Cataloging in Publication Data is available
ISBN 979-8-88966-145-0

Tripier, Perrine
Our Precious Wars

Cover design and illustration by Ginevra Rapisardi

Prepress by Grafica Punto Print – Rome

Printed in the USA

CONTENTS

OUR PRECIOUS WARS

Cool rain on a blue lawn. Damp summer grass, whiffs of black earth. Always these August showers falling on the closely-mown blades burned with gold. Heavy drops stream down the windowpane, meandering, snaking their way, weaving into long ribbons of liquid light. So many afternoons spent behind the gauze veil of curtain, fingers tracing their path, nervous and languid at the same time. Fine downy hair curling around my cheeks, and I'm surprised that it's so white, when I'm so young, radiant with light at the window. And suddenly my gaze drops from the window to the hand parting the curtains, and that hand is old, so old.

There are places that harpoon you. That coil their net around your dreams, that retract their claws just enough to let you grow up, but in your flesh they leave the scars of their ascendancy.

There are doors that let out a cry when they are opened, as if time has broken into forgetting, once again.

There are staircases I would so like to climb again, just once, to let the cool shine of the banister flow over my palm.

That is the House.

But then there are places that chill the back of your neck with the damp unease of the unfamiliar. Places that fail to resonate inside you. Places imposed on you, that you are forced to put up with, it's temporary, transitory, you have no choice.

When the world tires of you, you are offered the TV by the bed, the night table for your glasses case, and yellow wallpaper. Yellow is cheerful, and besides, you have everything you need here, you'll be looked after. You are made to swap the House for a room in a medically approved place where old people go to die. That yellow wallpaper—it's the blow of the bludgeon against my old neck.

Besides, the only thing I like now is the armchair. It's the only piece of furniture I was able to bring with me. It has always been an old person's armchair: it was my great-grandfather's, I didn't know him, and then it was my Great-Aunt Babel's, when she came to visit. I understand why a body comes to love it as one gets old; you find a kindred spirit in its dust, its softness. With my fingertip I worry the worn patches in the old rose velvet.

The comfort of settling one's arms into the intimacy of the armrest. The fabric rubs gently, like a second skin snuggling close. It's like finding the embrace of a sweet lover, one who has stayed far more constant than all the men I might have known.

When I think about it, I was the only one who really loved the House. Even my great-great-grandfather, who wanted it, imagined it, and built it, did not love it as much as I did. I loved it enough to stay there all my life. To give up my studies in the City, because it made me too unhappy to be so far away from the woods of my childhood. To say no to Oktav, when he held out the little ring on the Pont-Noir bridge one Wednesday afternoon, because he would never have agreed to live in the House. He wanted us to move into a large apartment in the old city center, not far from the secondary school where he would have been a teacher and where our future children would have learned to surpass us. I loved the House enough not to wish for anything else my whole life long, other than to stay there, nestled in the hollow of familiar things, to submit to the burnishing of time, just like the banister on the spiral staircase.

I always close my eyes when I want to remember. I do it every day, every moment of consciousness, perhaps. I struggle, impatiently, sometimes even violently, to re-create every room, every nook. I cling to details, to the shape of the light switches, the sound of the door handles as they are pressed, the fine film of dust on the yellow lightbulbs. I want to hollow out the space of the present and, with the power of frenzied memories, bring back the places I loved so much, which I knew by heart, which I walked through all my life and which, now that I am no longer there, are fading, disintegrating.

I do remember the House as I left it, the House of four, maybe five, months ago. I remember it a bit too well, even. The slow decline of the deserted rooms, the scuffed parquet floors, the cold corridors where the paint was peeling: that I do remember. The broken pane in the stained-glass window that allowed dead leaves to blow in, and swirl feebly across the floor of the entrance hall like a couple waltzing exhausted at the end of the night—that I can still see, and very clearly. And the faded white cast-iron radiators, too, icy to the touch in rooms where no one lives anymore—fireplaces walled up, dust sheets covering the furniture in rooms where no one sleeps anymore. That's how it was, at the end.

I want to banish that image of the House. To revive the colors, throw open the clear windows and let the intoxicating morning air rush in, wax the staircase, clean the huge dining room table. Lay out place settings for a dozen people or more, like in the heyday when everyone came, without exception.

I want to see the tall white wooden House, how when we came in from the garden it would suddenly appear, nestled among the tall blue spruces and the maple trees, with the grass parting in bursts of emerald on either side of the steps leading up to the entrance. To see the façade with its narrow windows, and the veranda jutting out on the left-hand side, and the high pointed roof spiked with chimneys and immaculately white gables, and the oeil-de-boeuf in the attic gazing out like the round, bright eye of a reassuring giant, trimmed with sculpted wood all around. I want to see the strange sharp roofs again, how they covered the bow-windows and were fringed in winter with icicles. I want to see the windows glistening in the cool air again, caressed whenever a gentle breeze blew through the branches of the trees that had grown too near the House. I want to see the big House again, with its ornate wooden pillars framing the entrance, and their warm varnish of solid caramel, and the stained glass window of intertwining flowers which, when the sun shone through it, caused shards of color to filter into the hall. The hall itself, painted with a huge trellis of tropical foliage, glowed a soft blue. From there the spiral staircase wound its way upwards in a whirlwind of coppery wood.

Everything was open, and smells from the kitchen would waft out unrestricted, permeating the entire House. From the salon to the attic, voices murmured, like a restful mountain stream flowing within the walls. Deep in my ears I can still hear it. The parquet creaks and gives off a scent of pine, and even the lightest of our childhood footsteps causes the thick floorboards to moan. We run up the staircase, because it's more fun to feel dizzy when you reach the top. The corridor on the first floor leads to the rooms that were our aunt's and uncle's when they were small, and which they still occupy when they come back to visit with our cousins. And those cousins sleep directly across from the bedroom I share with Harriett. It's more practical for playing, they have only to cross the corridor and whisper the password at the door to let us know that they're not bothersome grownups come to scatter everything with their long clumsy legs. At the very end of the corridor there's a bathroom, the green one, with its window that squeaks a little, but which overlooks part of the orchard. Opposite, there is Great-Aunt Babel's room, for when she comes for a visit, her trunks oozing camphor. When they've all gone away again, we have almost the whole floor to ourselves. We can't really play on the second floor, it's our parents' floor, and it's a serious place, with the two most spacious bathrooms. Lastly, lucky Louisa has her own bathroom, with a little porcelain tub behind her wardrobe. Because she's the eldest daughter, she has the biggest bedroom all to herself. But I wouldn't swap my room with her for anything on earth, because if I did, Harriett and I would no longer be able to make so much noise, given how near we would be to our parents' room. That's also where the storage room is, which we no longer even use for games of hide-and-seek: we know only too well that it's the first place anyone thinks of when it's time to hide. The best hiding place is, naturally, the attic. It's not as big as when Petit Père was a boy because since then they've divided it in two, to make a garret room for Klaus. I like Klaus's room. It smells of boy, because he doesn't open the window very often. And as the grownups never go up there, no one bothers us. We can hear how the roof creaks on stormy nights, and there's something so comforting about being in that warm attic room; like a cocoon of wood hanging above the forest.

But the images reel past in faded colors, emptied of life. Faces are blurred, and that's the most painful thing of all, to realize that the image of my family, young and alive, has been lost forever. And I have been lost. Who was I at the age of eight? Now that old age bends my back and twists my fingers, I can sense how annoyed I would have been, as a child, by the person I am now, encumbered by everything that no longer exists. I would have hated this puppet theater I constantly evoke to replay dead images. Who were we, in the woods and in our bedrooms, in the kitchen where the soup is steaming? I manipulate the marionettes, and their faces vanish. It doesn't matter, there comes a time when some have become so familiar that we no longer even need their physical presence for them to be there. We can only say we truly know someone when we've grown up with them. Our individual development has been lightly colored by that of others, like water into which a drop of syrup has fallen, a single drop, enough to color the entire glass a pale mint. I know exactly what Petit Père or Louisa would have made of such a comment, I can still see Petite Mère's smile when she watched us dance on a spring evening. And so, I sense that, for a while, in the body I have today, this awkward creaking body, I'm reliving the days that ended and the days that followed, in the depths of the House.

I want to remember the glorious children's voices as our limbs tangled together, Petit Père's cold, modest affection, Petite Mère's bursts of inspiration when she suddenly sprang up from the table, grabbed her brushes from the jar on the buffet, and rushed out to her studio in a corner of the veranda. I want to remember when Klaus, Louisa, and Harriett were still at the House, and Klaus was already on the threshold of adolescence. He was handsome, my big prodigy of a brother, brilliant, funny, insolent with talent. I wish I could complain, once again, about his playing one scale after the other at six o'clock in the morning, the sweet, hoarse lament of his trumpet waking the entire household. I want to see Louisa again, the loveliest of the daughters. It was as if she had absorbed all our mother's radiance, leaving none for Harriett or me. I remember how I would go up to the second floor and drag my feet along the parquet past Louisa's half-open door, and she was neither on her bed nor in her armchair but always at her bathroom mirror, gazing into her own eyes, searching for specks of gold deep in her iris.

What I would give to see the room again, with its two little beds side-by-side, Harriett's and mine, and the lamp in the middle, the cause of so many fights between us, because I always wanted to read later into the night than she did. To see her sly little baby face before she hid under the comforter, shouting that I was keeping her from getting her eight hours' sleep. "Then don't get up so early," I would say, jubilantly, turning the pages of my novel ever so slowly to enrage her all the more. "You know very well that Klaus will wake us up with his stupid trumpet, so switch off the light!" she protested, indignant, her eyes welling with tears as she punched her pillow. "I'll switch off when I've finished my chapter." "Show me how far you've got." I showed her the wrong page, deliberately. "You see, I'm almost done," I assured her. She began hissing like a snake, I was a liar, I was the worst sister ever, just wait until she told Louisa . . . She let the threat hang over me and shot me a furious look from under the sheets. Harriett constantly turned to our older sister to put an end to our quarrels, because Louisa was absolutely partial and unjust. She always sided with Harriett, who had adorable dark curls that Louisa loved to style, whereas my mop, she said, was "perplexifying." But since Harriett was anything but docile, most of the time Louisa went out slamming the door and seeking refuge in her own room to dream of chandeliers and dinners among friends.

Even the House of my adolescent years: I wish I could see it. The House that haunted me every night in my student lodgings, and which made me hate the Collège and curse my studies. They had torn me from my home, from my life, from my walks in the woods and my afternoons reading curled up on the too-hard window ledge. But the elation of Friday evenings! I hurried to the train, leapt onto my seat, fidgeted with impatience, and then my lips spread wide in an irrepressible grin, as the inexorable machine carried me far away from the towers of the City. How I loved that moment of arrival at the station, although it seemed endless until we got there, then seeing Petit Père by the open trunk that was just waiting for my suitcase, with Harriett already there in the car, because she finished earlier on Fridays.

"Madame Aberfletch? Can you hear me? I'm putting your tray on the desk, you can eat when you like."

And here's the cheery nurse who comes and dispels everything with her rose-scented perfume. She can go to hell with her white coat and insolent youth, that limpid voice of hers, a lively young woman who goes home in the evening. She must yearn for summer all year long, that season of melting bodies, and endless sunlit evenings.

Summer

There was nothing I liked better than summer at the House. Everything was radiant, in the muggy languor of vacations that seemed endless, drawn out by long days of delicious ennui. With the first heat of June everything began to sparkle, to brim with life. The maples and spruces seemed to overflow with an incandescent sap; the grass was a brash green, splashed with vast sheets of sunlight.

Everyone returned from the City, flooding back toward the familiar countryside, to forests suffused with lustrous shade. You had only to stand at the edge of the woods to feel the resin-scented wind exhale its murmur. When we were children, my father's brother and sister, Uncle Bertie and Aunt Hilde, came every summer with their families. Such joy when we were told, "Your cousins will be here this evening!" The day was suddenly filled with impatient agitation, as we hopped in circles around the salon, and when Petit Père scolded us, back up the staircase we'd go, stifling our nervous laughter. The afternoon was spent in a flurry of preparations; I loved helping my parents, with painstaking attention. Like a petty despot I took care that the attic had been aired out, that the toy chests were open, and that the sheets had been carefully folded on the beds. I went tearing down the spiral staircase, waxed for the occasion; I whirled around the entrance hall where the crushed light of the stained-glass window fell. I went twenty times or more into the kitchen, leaned over the stove, breathed in the fumet as I raised the lid of each soup tureen with a trembling hand. I knew that this was the signal, when the food was almost ready: our cousins would be here any minute, and in no time we would all be sitting at the table together amid an unbearable hubbub of loud laughter, releasing the frenzy of a long day's waiting.

The evening our cousins arrived, every year in early summer, was always the same. As a rule, they were exhausted from their day on the road—the hot breath of tar, the stifling closeness of traffic, the sun reflected on the bright surface of the car. But still we gathered eagerly around the table. When everything seemed to be dancing with light and laughter and pleasant smells, when we were constantly interrupted in our storytelling by a dish being passed around, or another story suddenly being told at the other end of the table, and when I leaned back in my chair to examine furtively everyone we hadn't seen since Christmas, I was as if plunged in a bath of liquid joy, golden and sparkling, fragrant with the scent of honey from Uncle Bertie's cigars, or the thyme permeating the juice from the chicken. My gaze circled the table, moving automatically over familiar faces, to catch on those of my girl cousins, ever prettier with each passing year. I was fascinated more than anything by their nose, small and round, which came from Bertie's in-laws. He had not been spared our family nose, long and hooked, where light glided as if on a blade. Amelia and Magda took after their mother in every way, a sort of fair, fleshy grace, the skin below their neck all rosy, a skin of fresh petals pearling with water in crystal-clear vases. Always seated side by side, cautiously passing the pitcher when it was placed before them, they laughed wholeheartedly at all of Klaus's or Harriett's pranks. Every summer, as soon as the two cousins had climbed out of the car and set foot on the steps up to the entrance, they would look Louisa up and down, as she did them. In the first moments of their reunion we were never certain they wouldn't tear each other to pieces or exchange the typical catty remarks pretty girls make; on the contrary, they fell into each other's arms and went into the House, laughing, leaving in their wake a scent of precious oils. Harriett and I didn't spend much time with these cousins, who were the same age as Louisa and similar in character. We were little pests, noisy and rather troublesome, I believe. Klaus showed no particular interest in his cousins and sat at the table next to Aleksander, my aunt Hilde's beloved son. In addition to the typical Aberfletch nose, Aleksander had a steel gaze which clashed with the murky-pond depths of our own eyes. His hair was lighter, more ashen than ours, and he held his head very straight, catching the light from the dining room lamp, which cast its warm glow over the entire table. Aleksander and Klaus didn't really get on all that well, but as they were the eldest children, they had learned to coexist in a sort of defiant brotherhood, halfway between rivalry and solidarity. They vied in dexterity when it came to pouring the water, to see who could raise the pitcher highest without the fine flow of water straying from its course. We applauded, staring as the troubled water quickly filled the glass, and shouted the moment it was about to spill over.

The grownups were nervous and sent us to bed early, telling us not to "carry on until all hours like last year." We exchanged gleeful gazes with the cousins at that point, our complicity suddenly revived by that reminder of a shared past. For a split second memories bathed in summer light streamed past our inner gaze, trembling with laughter and scraped knees. We went up to our cousins' room with them, dancing, so excited to have them here again, and Klaus acted the "eldest" and said, with a growl of his fine voice, which was in the process of changing, "I'm going up to my room. Behave yourselves, kids." Aleksander seemed a little put out: although he was the same age as Klaus, he was obliged to share a room with his girl cousins, whom he cheerfully ignored most of the time. Louisa and

Klaus disappeared into the gloom of the stairway, and Harriett, our cousins, and I stood in the dark corridor of neutral territory between our two bedrooms. We were so glad to see their suitcases through the half-open door, miraculously brought up by a devoted parent; they now lay on their respective beds in the yellow lamplight. This room was empty all year round, the bed bases cold and bare, except when our cousins came. We got out huge clean sheets for them, still smelling of the lavender scattered throughout the wardrobes. On the first evening the cousins still looked tired, but seemed truly happy to be back. Harriett and I stood in their doorway, watching as they ran to the window, as if to make sure the view hadn't changed since the previous summer. Then, satisfied, they rubbed their eyes, yawned, and wished us good night. I took Harriett forcefully by the shoulder to lead her back into our room, because she was far too wound up to sleep, and wanted to play, right now—hide-and-seek in the dark, or spy on the grownups, or sneak up on Klaus in his garret, creeping ever so quietly up the stairs so they wouldn't creak. I told her we had every evening, all summer long, to play, and she came along, her resignation tinged with delight.

As I lay in bed staring up at the ceiling, now veiled in blue shadow, I felt the weight of the two floors above me, and I could sense the busyness of the grownups as they cleared the table below us, with the warm murmuring of their husky voices. I listened to the night noises of bedtime preparations, Louisa upstairs walking hurriedly from her bathroom to her bed, the cousins on the other side of the corridor putting their things away in wardrobes, disembarking, settling in, taking possession once again of the room they came to every summer. I felt part of a whole, now, surrounded by the people I loved, and the House, full at last with this large family who shared my blood, had truly come alive. I knew it wasn't such a bad thing, that we'd gone to bed a little early tonight, because there would be other evenings. Harriett always ended up breaking the silence, her husky little voice saying, "Isn't it great the cousins are here." Any other night I would have told her to be quiet, because I didn't feel like talking. But there I was, curled up in my sheets, and the summer breeze was blowing gently against the shutters. So I answered, simply, "Yes it's really great." We talked about what we'd do the following day. In the near total obscurity of the room, all I could see of Harriett was a dark little mass on the pillow swollen with a lighter shadow, enormous in comparison to her head. This was my favorite moment of the day, the flow of promises, plans, and ideas made even wilder because they were already mingling with a semi-conscious store of dreams. We slipped into silence, like a flash of light on the surface of a pond, and waves of sleep closed over our eyes.

We let the days flow past like a stream of liquid light. It was a precious time of yielding hours, evanescent mornings, endless afternoons.

The morning was always a time for each of us to be alone. You could hardly tell anyone else lived in the House, we were all so silent, with the closed doors of those who were sleeping in, the empty salon still smelling of Bertie's honey cigars.

I always woke before Harriett, because my bed was closer to the window, and a ray of white sunlight filtered through the slits in the shutters to mark out a warm spindle on my sheets. I stayed there for a few minutes, but then I heard the birds outside, the confused buzzing of wasps against the window frame, and I had a certain mad urge to look at the garden, to see the sparkling morning lawn spread wide before my gaze, and to feel the glorious breeze billowing my dress. So as to avoid waking Harriett, I didn't open the shutters. My eyes, which had adjusted to the pale shadow could easily make out the obstacles between my bed and the door. I slowly made my way out of the room, careful not to cause the floor to creak. My toes first encountered the hard solid floor, then the scratchy carpet that tickled the soles of my feet. I cautiously avoided the sharp corners of our beds, the toy chest, and the wardrobe, and I glanced anxiously at the little round form curled beneath her flowered comforter, to make sure she hadn't moved. Then I put one hand on the door handle, the other on the latch, and I pulled abruptly, so that the door wouldn't groan—a poorly oiled door always makes more noise when you open it slowly. The morning light flooding the corridor left me unsteady for a moment. The row of closed doors intimidated me, made it impossible to tell whether I was the first one up or not. Still rather dazed, I went down the staircase. There, too, I had to avoid causing the wood to squeal, to be careful where I put my feet, choosing certain steps over others, so I took giant steps, clinging to the banister to keep my balance. It was the first adventure of the day, to be repeated every morning.

When I went through the deserted hall, the foliage appeared terrifying now as the morning light cast a cold shimmer. The painted flowers looked smudged, like ancient stars disappearing. The tiles were always freezing, and I hurried on to the kitchen. There the clock was ticking, and it was the only moment of the day I noticed it, because the rest of the time its mechanical pulsing was hidden by the sounds of the House—the laughter, voices, discordant clatter of pots and pans being put away. The kitchen was cool, the windows and shutters had been left open onto the garden to allow the night air to circulate. In the morning, we had to banish the bark-colored moths that had slipped in to huddle against the walls for warmth. They flew about clumsily, unable to find the way out, and their trembling wings flapped against the window panes.

I closed the windows, biting my lip when they banged, rather loudly. The dishes by the sink had dried, and a puddle of cold water was dripping from the edge to the drain. I loved the kitchen windows, with their little white frames that looked out onto the waking orchard. I hoisted myself up onto the counter top, cluttered with jars and spatulas, and pressed my nose against the pane. Through the vapor of my breath I observed the vague outlines of the trees heavy with fruit. Timid emerald leaves quivered in the sun like little green-veined fish.

I went into the salon, then the library, both deserted, and already I sighed with boredom. Honestly, the grownups were just too lazy, sleeping like this when the day was already on its way; it wouldn't wait. Suddenly, I hear something moving overhead. Light slippers, making the parquet creak—now the game is to guess who it is. If they come down the staircase quickly, it will be Harriett or Klaus. Our cousins come down quickly too, but not as quickly as us, especially the first few days; they have to get used again to certain tricky steps with shiny wood. A slow, heavy step, that will be Uncle Bertie. In the morning Bertie smells incredibly nice, because he always has his bath before coming down, and once I saw him generously splashing eau de Cologne onto his freshly shaven neck with the palm of his hand. The skin under his chin turns red and shiny, blooming in his wake is the smell of tall grasses swaying in the wind.

Then, gradually, the entire House was astir, stretching, yawning, throwing open all the windows onto the garden. The wind caused the white sheets to billow, and scattered pollen onto pillows. Our cousins came down one after the other, their little faces still drowsy, with crease marks from the sheets on their warm cheeks, and Aleksander with his coarse flaxen hair tufting on his brow. The grownups let their large, evanescent presence drift around the kitchen sink, busily passing bowls to each other as they discussed how they'd slept. Hilde always complained a little because the bed springs squeaked, and Bertie said he slept very well, as he pinched Suzy's waist, his "Little Lady" with her rosebud face. Breakfast for us was hastily dispatched, no time to lose, you've slept enough you lazy lot, the garden awaits, we have loads of cabins to build in masses of trees thronged with birds. It was as if my lungs, filled with the morning air, had given my voice greater resonance and, with the help of my faithful first mate Harriett, we very quickly aroused the enthusiasm of the entire gang, and were already inventing a host of projects, while our parents were having coffee that was already too hot for this balmy morning. A dash of cold water on our faces by the sink, then the rallying cries, as we bent over the banister: "Everyone to the garden!" "Where's Klaus?, " "Already in the shed?," "And what are Amelia and Magda up to?"

The way we could run! A swarm of curls bobbing in the sun, always taking the same path; the same enchantment seized us every morning, at the same hour of the vast blue sky. We scrambled out the front door, pushing it open with our little hands still pale with early summer, and we leapt down all the steps in one bound. On landing in the soft grass we were once again in contact with the earth. A new impulse, and down the verdant slope we charged. Long blades of grass tore at our ankles, clung to our calves, and grasshoppers leapt around us in a chaotic jig. The edge of the forest: we held our breath. The shade was blue, and the first rays of sunlight angled through the leaves with gold. There was a lovely smell of resin, that fine resin that has distilled all night into a nectar of sap. Klaus ran fastest. Harriett was hot on our heels, she did her best but she was little, and as she ran she shrieked at the top of her lungs. Magda, Amelia, and Louisa hopped along like nymphs, as if setting garlands of pearls on the moss that brushed against their feet. That was their role, in fact, to decorate each new cabin, each rough wooden shelter. "They have good taste," our parents often said, heartened by their grace, reassured of their future ease in finding husbands and having children.

It was always Klaus and Aleksander who chose the copse.

For several years we'd settled in the same group of trees with low-hanging branches that had little moss on them and offered plenty of irregularities for handholds and footholds, with very dark blue leaves that always looked polished with frost. We went back there every day—even when we were on the lookout for other spots—to vary a bit, to expand our colony, explore the world, and have an emergency shelter in the event of an attack, a storm, or a solar explosion. Our main cabin was built a little like the House. A very pointed roof, very high. The first summer or two we could all stand inside it, then Klaus and Aleksander grew taller, and in any case they wanted to have their own private cabins, for boys, far away from the girls. It took them a summer or two to secede from us, and, paradoxically, those were the most thrilling summers of our entire childhood. Abandoned, left behind, we girls had to take things in hand and share our tasks in order to protect our territory from the boys, who hid in the surrounding bushes to frighten us, to steal our sticks and ropes and flat stones. Harriett and I were the scouts. It was far and away the most exciting role, but also the most terrifying. Hearts racing as we crouched behind a tree in order to glance over our shoulders. Incandescent warriors, amazon queens with fiery manes, spear in hand, dagger at our thigh, we were as silent and supple as panthers as we crept through the forest, our fingers tense around our grubby dew-laced sticks. Our mission was to locate the new cabin the boys had built and, if need be, destroy their base, to force them back into the ranks. Amelia kept watch, because she was tall and could stay up in a tree for hours, fiddling with her hair. Moreover, she had a piercing cry; we'd had ample opportunity to hear it. Louisa was in charge of provisioning and liaising with the House. She saw to the wood supply, should we want to enlarge the cabin, or make repairs after nights of strong wind. As for Magda, she proclaimed herself princess of the forest and wandered among the trees, grandiloquent and sovereign, a crown of lichen woven into her blond hair. When we came back empty-handed with Harriett, after we'd scoured every corner of the forest, or so it seemed, we all made an effort to do without the boys, and our excitement waned. We were just a bit weary of staying in this chilly forest where the sun filtered so reluctantly, and we began to dream of the lovely warmth that must be glazing the vegetable garden or the veranda, back there by the House. And besides, we missed the boys. It was different when they were there, reassuring us with their piercing, chivalrous cries, their sturdy calves and the faint, fair down on their tanned arms. We felt we were all part of a harmonious tribe, where everyone had their place. Deep down, we didn't like this sedition business.

All our rituals, all our songs have been forgotten. We should have written them down in a notebook, I should have had it here, in a drawer, and I could have taken it out, to immerse myself even deeper in those golden woods, when we were ten years old. I remember a few things, childhood refrains, vague and distant like a cowbell at the far end of a meadow. Oh yes, it smells of pigs in Klaus's digs, we sang. Children are relentless: I think that's what we sang whenever we went up to Klaus's garret room. It smells of pigs in Klaus's digs, Harriett adored saying it, she thought it was fabulous, very well put, it sounded terrific. We had our own special little expressions; they lasted a few months then vanished. As adolescents we brought them up again, gushing, Remember what we used to sing to Klaus, when we were little, and we'd try it again, to make our big brother laugh. One summer the cousins had a tune in their heads, some current hit, and everyone vaguely made fun of the singer's voice, as croaky as a frog's, but we all ended up humming the tune to ourselves. It would just be there, without warning, when we were washing our hands, for example. Our gaze lost in the stream of water over our soapy fingers, we'd catch ourselves by surprise, humming that silly tune.

What has the nurse brought me on her tray? They do make an effort in the kitchen, I won't deny it. The meat is good, but then the pasta is never cooked enough. You can tell, after all, when noodles aren't cooked. They lack that translucent, melt-in-your-mouth softness. I have a backache from sitting in this armchair. I ought to go for a walk along the corridor. But if it's to run into people . . . I may as well stay here. People in retirement homes are always very distant. Old people, like you yourself, already have an entire life behind them, but lack the strength or memory to tell the story. And besides, you don't feel like explaining to a stranger why you didn't marry Oktav. They'll only judge you, those who have three children—who never come to see them, to be sure, but their smiling faces do at least adorn the bedside table. Is Oktav dead? He had the most beautiful eyes, and it was ever so hard, afterwards, to think of those moist irises brimming with emerald. He liked my eyes very much, too. They're murky-pond eyes, I replied, every time. "Then you must not have seen very many lovely ponds in your life," he said. I told him I'd grown up in a huge House with a forest and a vegetable garden, and a lake full of water lilies between the rushes and the dragonflies; told him that I missed the House, that I would give anything to go back there rather than continue my studies in the City, rather than have a profession, a husband, children. That for a single water lily from the lake I would give a thousand Oktavs. He looked sad, and I liked that. We couldn't have gotten married.

I think it all started with the book I always had with me for the slack hours in summer, when everything was drowsing in the sun after lunch. It was rest time. You mustn't make any noise, not a sound, while on every floor of the House the grownups were lying lethargically in their rooms with gauzy muslin curtains. "The wine goes to your head when you drink during the day," Aunt Hilde moaned, in protest. So they all lay down, and we were confined to absolute peace and quiet. We were not allowed to go out during those hours, the hottest of the day, hours of molten lead which liquefied our legs. Our cousins followed Louisa up to her room and they played quietly at dressing up, parading in front of the mirror. Klaus and Aleksander also went upstairs to talk in the restful shade of the attic, breathing the dust of the sun as it floated in under the roof structure. Harriett was always immeasurably fatigued after the meal, and her little legs, which had trotted so valiantly all morning, aspired to nothing more than resting on a cool mattress. I, therefore, was generally alone from lunch until three o'clock, and the convulsive azure sky trembled in the heat when I placed my forehead against the window. Banished from my room, where Harriett was sleeping, obliged to avoid any creaking corridors so as to not wake the snoring grownups, and the salon because Petit Père lay there on the sofa, and the kitchen because the sweltering heat came in through every window with the saturated air of the sun at its zenith, so I wandered from room to room, feeling weak and weary. Those were the best hours for reading. Most often I would slip onto the seat in the bow window in Petit Père's study, making the most of his absence. It smelled of hot leather, and the mahogany desk shone in a single ray of sunlight, sparkling with gold like a piece of honeycomb. I pressed myself against the warm windowpane, my hair rubbing against the wooden wall. There I would read. I nearly always read the same book when I was little, or at any rate I re-read it every summer, because its pages fed my dreams and inspired my bursts of creativity in the woods. The cover was scarlet, as rough as snakeskin, and etched with glittering letters. The book was gilt-edged, and for a long time I let the early afternoon sunlight play over the pages, as fine and transparent as a dragonfly's wings. *Secret Glory*, was the title. By Amber Gardano. It was the story of a princess, or a queen, or an empress who, for some obscure reason to do with keeping her kingdom whole and to herself alone, refuses to marry any of the princes her councilors present to her. She spends the entire novel fleeing from one tower of the castle to another, in order to avoid her ministers' reproaches. Leaning out the window of the dungeon where she has sought refuge, she relishes in her solitude as she gazes at the expanse of her undivided realm. She repeats that no one on earth deserves to stride through the vast rooms of her castle, that she alone loves it and knows its true worth. I think my entire character was formed by reading these pages, as I devoured them all through the torpid July hours.

I eventually emerged dazed from so much reading, drowning my eyes in the vibrant white pages; I let the book slip to the far end of my perch, and my feet felt sticky on the warm parquet floor. It was time to go and wake the lazybones. There began a quest as irritating as it was delightful, since the time spent searching every floor of the House to find out where the others were playing meant there was that much less time to devote to our shared games. I began with my cousins, half-opening their door like a little spy, holding my breath. Imagine my disappointment when I saw the beds were empty, and had hastily been made. I rushed into our room. If Harriett was no longer there, a terrible anxiety came over me: it meant they had, no doubt, all gone off to play without me. They were all running and messing around in the tall grasses, building fabulous tree houses in the new trees they'd discovered at the edge of the woods without me, without me, leaving me alone in a House full of snoring grownups. When this happened I was so panicked at the thought of missing out, of failing to be in on an adventure that would go on to feed their mischievous innuendos at dinner that evening, and I wouldn't know what they were talking about, that I no longer paid any attention at all to the sound of my footsteps on the parquet floor. I ran breathlessly from one floor to the next, careening down the staircase, murmuring their names to myself in fury, then suddenly I came upon them calmly putting on their shoes in the hall, or looking for tools in the shed. And then a great beam of warmth would light up my mind, as the hank of anxiety gradually unwound; my moment of distress was coming to an end. I had found them, and laughing serenely they said, "We looked everywhere for you, we thought you were already in the cabin!" Just to know they hadn't forgotten me, that they'd even looked for me, just to feel Harriett's nervous little arm curl around mine, and to meet my cousins' familiar gaze immediately restored my feeling of plenitude. And off we ran, again.

Our perfect freedom as children was in no way restricted by the proximity of grownups. On the whole they found us coarse, inconsequential, and badly brought up, and whenever we went near them in the garden they scolded us; their mouths were always thick with reproach. We were covered in dust, pink in the face and damp with sweat, and our vitality clashed with their unhealthy sluggishness, their endless daytime siestas. Just by running in the distance we wore them out, and they exasperated us by leaving their shutters half-closed in the very middle of the afternoon. We didn't say a word to them all day, we were too busy running from the orchard to the staircase, leaping from one room to the next, our arms filled with sheets, ropes, boards; we burst from the woods singing at the top of our lungs. We didn't even see them; at best they vaguely got in the way as we tore through the House, and to us they seemed slow, heavy, and tiresome. It was the same phenomenon at mealtimes, and while they spoke loudly and shouted now and then when one of us clumsily dropped a piece of cutlery into our plates, and the dissonant clatter recalled our existence to them, we were actually still just as isolated as we'd been in any of the cabins we'd been building all day long. Petit Père complained at dinner because we hadn't come down as promptly as he'd like us to. But when Bertie cupped his giant hands around his mouth, we instantly interrupted our games: his booming voice carried more authority than Petit Père's, and crackled with the warmth of a good fire, was as vibrant as a hunter's horn, and always placed everyone in agreement.

They had us sit at the end of the table, so we'd be on our own. We had our particular way of passing the food along. Children don't speak much among themselves; they *show*, above all. Little hands tracing golden signs in the air, galloping along the table, twirling the corks left next to the grownups' bottles, with varying degrees of skill. Chubby fingers intertwining and competing to create alignments of crumbs on the table. Between the half-empty plates and the base of the clear glasses sparkling in the lamplight, we reconstructed the garden and the forest: the orchard over there, the House here. While our parents raved about what was on the table—the quality of the *jarret*, the spices in the wine, the soft fresh texture of the bread—we were transforming the space into a concentration of the days' dreams. We were re-creating the place where we wanted to be at that moment, rather than sitting there starched with clothes made of thick fabric, "because the evening air is chilly."

Summer was the time when our cousins became siblings, and the identity of our parents merged with that of our uncles and aunts. The family was recomposed, Petit Père and Petite Mère were strangers to me now, almost shadowy figures in a House that no longer belonged to them, and no longer belonged to us, either. Those empty rooms that suddenly came to life—bathrooms always occupied, doors left open the rest of the year now bolted shut: this left us feeling delightfully dispossessed. The House had not fundamentally changed, it was simply that we saw it differently. When our cousins were there, when all the rooms were occupied, and damp towels were set out here and there to dry, their soapy smell not the one we were used to, I felt both lost and serene. From time to time, especially in the evening before turning in at the end of the meal, Petite Mère would grab me by the arm and ask for a hug, something I would have gladly given her the rest of the year, but which now had to be coaxed from me, because she was no longer my mother, just one grownup among others. When she paused in her dishwashing as I went by, and my arms went mechanically around her neck in the gloom of the kitchen, I was surprised, as if roused from a dream where I was drowning, and only regained my wits when my nose, struggling for air, broke through the surface of the water. I suddenly remembered that I was not a fierce warrior woman but a little girl, and this woman who smelled so sweetly of orange flower and almond, holding me against her light hair in the kitchen, was my mother, on whose lap I'd curl up quite naturally in winter, on the sofa. It lasted only a few seconds, the length of a hug, then she murmured in my ear, "Off you go, go join your cousins, have fun."

The absolute freedom of those summer days is what set that season apart from the rest of the year. The delight of those balmy blue evenings when we ate outside, under the tall cedar tree. Sustained whiffs of resin drifted over the long table. Tiny insects sometimes fell from the low-lying branches above our heads. They would try to flee, wriggling away from Harriett's quick fist. The grownups seemed more faraway than ever, their voices borne away on the wind. The long outline of their figures blurred in the violet shadow, their reddish profiles dimly lit by the quivering warmth of the lanterns. Whenever we ate outside they spent their time complaining—which explains why it happened so rarely. Nothing was as it should be, the wind blew the tablecloth into Hilde's knees, the benches were too hard, the mosquitoes were annoying, the kitchen was too far away when it came time to clear the table. And we rejoiced to hear them moaning like that, because our favorite game, as soon as we'd finished our plates, was to disappear into the gloom of the trees and carry out secret missions, without our parents noticing that we'd left the table. Nothing could be more intoxicating than to run off laughing into the night as it crackled with crickets and dried thorns. And for us to dash as fast as possible without looking back, until we were in among the trees that sprang from the shadow, and we leapt blindly above the bushes and the rocks to feel the soft carpet of silent moss beneath our feet. We were proud warriors, quick and agile among the trees, invisible in the cool night. Our hearts beat even faster than usual, a rapid pulsing of vigorous young blood, of blood nourished by trivial fears and great plans. When it seemed to us that we were far enough away, we stopped, one by one, and we counted to see who we might have lost on the way. It was always Magda who was frightened and stopped at the edge of the woods, then returned sheepishly to sit with the grownups. We walked slowly back to the tall cedar tree whose lanterns danced among the branches, and our parents' resounding laughter, reassuring now, guided us toward the warm flickering flames. Exhausted from inhaling the wind all day long, heady with this last escapade, we were shivering now that the heat of the sun, which had bathed our skin in a coppery steam, had been drawn away by the metallic glow of the moon. We walked quickly across the silvery lawn toward the bright windows of the House, went slowly up the staircase, and back to our respective beds, yawning a barely conscious good night.

Sometimes we didn't go to bed right away. The scent of the sun, our oily skin and tired gazes, our hoarse voices in the dark of the attic, where we gathered on the occasional evening after our games of hide-and-seek, have permeated the attic rooms for me forever. We'd sit on the rough, dusty floorboards where tiny termites ran along the cracks, and Klaus and Aleksander always found a way to show off by perching on a chest or a trunk that would make horrible creaking noises. Once one of them even gave way under Klaus's imposing behind, and his brown curls vanished in a cloud of dust while we all burst into rather terrified laughter.

Our tongues loosened in the attic. The funniest thing is that I have no idea what we could have been talking about during our febrile nocturnal whispering, in the glow of a flashlight wedged between two large hat boxes. We all spoke at the same time, describing, I suppose, our year so far and all our schoolyard exploits—the boys our female cousins had crushes on, the punishments Klaus and Aleksander had proudly amassed, as if they constituted so many elements proving their manliness. And the half-darkness of the attic, the long shadows projected by the flashlight's amber beam, the stacks of boxes and suitcases we could barely make out in the gloom, and all the furtive little night noises stimulated our imagination and aroused a certain fear. We tried to hide it from each other by speaking very quickly and leaving no room for silence, which was terrifying. Sometimes a cracking sound in the roof structure overhead or the patter of a mouse at the far end of the attic made us jump. We waited, breathlessly, eyeing each other until one of us identified the sound and reassured the others. That was frequently how the ghost story competition started between Klaus and Aleksander. Harriett and I managed quite well in our way, but our stories were not as frightening, because they were always tinged with magic or improbability. The one who, contrary to all expectations, had developed a real talent in the art, was Magda. Because she knew that her fair hair and the large bluish circles under her eyes made her resemble a young Victorian bride, she adopted a toneless voice, tilted her head slightly to one side, and with a wide, vacant gaze she explained how her four children had been found dead in the lake, or how she had heard moans coming from the bottom of a well of turbulent water. She was the scariest of all. She sometimes claimed she had lived long ago, that she'd been reincarnated to come and avenge her own death, which had, obviously, been atrocious and unjust. When Harriett began to fidget and crumple her night gown, hardly proud of herself, wrapping her arms around her knees, Louisa would call out loudly for the storytelling to cease at once. The boys sighed, and it generally ended up in a furious, whispered row, and we all went back to our rooms, where I had to see to Harriett, who had gone quite pale and would give a start at the slightest creak of the staircase.

To be honest, now that I recall that time, I don't think the days were as free as all that. The hours spent in the woods seem to have lasted forever, transfixed in the summer light. Time crawled over the dry moss at the foot of the tall trees. And yet I think that now and then we must have been requisitioned for various chores in the House—to carry a basket of washing to the laundry room, help Petite Mère hang it up, with the huge sheets that flapped vaporous against the blue sky. I let myself be intoxicated by the smell of cleanliness: pale lavender, the scent of soap slipping through one's fingers onto the immaculate white surface of the sink. Aleksander and Klaus skillfully sneaked off, but the cousins were too slow and constantly failed to keep up with us. We had to tear along the lane to fetch the mail from the letter box, which was full of cockroaches hiding in the shadows, and plunge a hand into that tenebrous, creaking mouth, most often to withdraw a letter from Great-Aunt Babel, who assured us that her sea baths were doing her a world of good. She went for treatment at a spa two months in summer and three in winter, until toward the end she could no longer get around so easily. We suspected her of wanting to avoid family gatherings during the holidays. And yet she'd known her share of fancy receptions. High society, the flashy, refined crowd, laughter sparkling beneath chandeliers, and pearls glinting from the trains of gowns. Babel returned from her spa even more weary than when she set off, which confirmed our theory that she only went there to be on her own in a big, cool room at a hotel. She'd always avoided us, always avoided the House, until she was forced to stay a little longer, in her final years. Despite the affection I felt for this bold old woman who required champagne at every meal, Babel, to me, was the very archetype of renunciation. Renunciation of her land, her forest, her family. I failed to see how anyone could spend their entire life preferring a ballroom to the plush of a forest carpeted in moss.

This digression about Babel . . . I don't want to think about her, I want to think about my childhood summers at the House, that's it, that is what I want to relive, not the decrepitude of a lady in furs who inevitably reminds me of my own senility. Yes, I have to say it, my back aches, the upholstery is uncomfortable, my slippers are too tight. We were young, once, we ran everywhere. The grownups found it very useful to have a little army of servants to requisition. We really didn't care about news from Great-Aunt Babel. She was lost in the day's sun-filled worries. Because we also had to pick the cherry tomatoes and the raspberries and set the table, and the incursion of reality, of contingency, of what was almost trivial into our childhood daydreams seemed like an insult to our wild mystical world, inhabited by shamanic fantasies. What did we care about folds in the tablecloth, or respecting some schedule, or watering plants, or crumbs on the table, when we had a kingdom among the branches, a population of warlike ants with gleaming abdomens marching up and down the tree trunks, abysses of shadow beneath the roots and gems buried among the lichen? The orchard didn't interest us anymore in summer. We had taken great care of the garden in the spring, when my sisters and I had watched for every bud beneath leaves glistening with rain, but now it was as if the garden must submit to the blaze of warm breezes. The flowers are lovely at the end of winter, delicate and vivid in the blue grass, but they dry out and harden in the summer sun, lose their radiance, are nothing but vague bulges lost in the lawn buzzing with hundreds of honeybees and bumblebees, so bothersome when you want to run through the thickets. There is no more room for the docile adornment of fragile petals; summer is a time for adventure, for resin-scented shade, for crushed raspberries on fingertips, nibbled as we balance between the trees, and the leaves tickle our backs.

And then there was the week of the Great Whitening. For some strange reason it was always at the beginning of August, when the heat was most intense. This was the week, every year, when the entire family joined ranks to repaint the façades of the House, discolored over the year by freezing autumn mists, winter snows, and spring showers. Long planks were faded, yellowed, even completely peeled away where tree branches had scraped against them. It was a family pact: in summer, everyone came to spend luminous days at the House but, in return, they had to contribute to the upkeep with these few days of renovation work. The opening night of the Great Whitening week was always the same. Toward the end of the meal Petit Père would slowly rise from his chair and declare the week open. We applauded, even if deep down we all knew that this week was always the most trying of the summer. Not that painting the walls was an unpleasant task in itself, far from it, there was even a certain satisfaction to be had from seeing the bright new white replace the faded ecru. But the crushing heat, our time for play reduced to nil, and the constant presence of the grownups in this intergenerational chore made it tiresome. We mustn't drop the cans of fresh paint, with their pungent smell, or our brushes, or the ladder, or the scaffolding; the paint had to be evenly spread and very smooth, any drops had to be brushed in the direction of the grain of the wood, to respect the crevices; we had to point out any suspicious cracks, any traces of termites or rot, and take frequent refreshment breaks. I recall that it seemed like an insult to see Petite Mère, who was a genuine artist, slapping paint on the façade with a big flat brush. This was a job for the others to do, at least it should have been. For Bertie, red in the face, hunched over on the scaffolding with his big sweating shoulders, or his wife Suzy, so sweet and meticulous and self-effacing, or Aunt Hilde, so assiduous, painting without a smile and clenching her teeth, because already at the time she wanted to sell the place, but no one knew that yet. Everyone thought that this time spent painting was, in fact, yet another way to share, to unite around a simple, constructive task that allowed us to maintain the House in good condition. It's true that everyone did take part, in their way. The youngest among us saw to keeping the lemonade stand in constant supply, there at the foot of the scaffolding that Petit Père and Uncle Bertie climbed up every morning at dawn, opposite that day's façade. And that is how we slowly made our way around the House, section by section. The children were also in charge of making sandwiches for the workers. We had to keep the ice bucket filled at all times, because everything melted so quickly in the sun with the reflection of the immaculate white planks. The tart taste of lemon bursting in icy bubbles on our palate, the faint tinkling of ice cubes against the glass, the powerful smell of paint: it all made the sky spin in a strange spiral of azure, lacquered with translucent white. The bright green grass, which splattered our feet and tickled our eyes, was an invitation to rest, to lie back and contemplate the treetops for hours. Nothing makes you feel more alive than pressing your back against the ground and letting the blades of grass spring from the earth and mingle with your hair while your fingers dig into the friable flesh of the crust of things.

Yet again I realize this is not the child speaking. There's nothing left of the girl I was seventy or seventy-five years ago. The hardest thing is to admit that I've done nothing yet have changed so greatly. It is time that changes a human being, and we let ourselves be eroded, like a shore by a stream. Have I let myself be polished? What have I forgotten, what did I feel, I myself, still so similar and yet so indisputably other, as I slipped down on the grass to let the sky pour into my eyes? I remember wishing the blueness of the sky would so fill my eyes that they'd become just as azure, luminous with sunlight, and I was blinding myself for no good reason, desperately drowning my pupils in the incandescent ether.

These hands caressed the mossy trunks of pine trees in the woods, these feet ran agile and febrile among the bushes. They're no longer the same hands, the same feet. Restrained by slippers, squeezed into loafers, frozen through inaction. Is getting old not swapping one's living self for a self that's prepared to die? Exchanging vital fluid, mad ideas, the intoxication of the world for a gentle somnolence, a cocoon of morphine, salutary and soothing? And yet I know very well that I haven't run anywhere for many years, and the House had become a cross to bear, a repository for my pain and solitude, and in springtime the sun's rays hardly warmed the parquet floors, chilled through by the long winter. What would I be doing, if I were still there? I could only pace up and down those beloved corridors, dragging my feet; only see the woods from a distance, through the windows, since I no longer have the strength to set off adventurously and get lost there. I would I only partially feel at home, and is that not the ultimate death?

They've told me not to speak so loudly, yes alright, I'm the only one they hear at the other end of the corridor, yes, fine, it bothers the other residents, don't you see, it's time for the afternoon nap. But the nurses don't know the House, and besides, they're young. When the present is painful and the future is macabre, of course we will go looking within for the way to the past, we will immobilize our consciousness and row against the current of time. Don't expect an old person to rejoice in the falling darkness.

Summer evenings . . . the murmur of crickets rising from the depths of a sea of grass . . . To feel the light breeze emerging from the shadow of the pine forest, the sky gradually turning shades of indigo, a single drop of water and a brush dipped in ultramarine for the purplish pigment to spread in liquid veins across the white paper . . .

We sat on the freshly painted porch in front of the veranda, with the garden sloping gently down to the orchard. We gazed at the treetops as they sharpened to black against a sky tinged gold. In the House, a clatter of pots and pans—they were preparing dinner, everyone was busy, Aunt Hilde's firm, deep voice winding around Petite Mère's lilting tones. Louisa and the cousins were getting changed upstairs, removing their dusty daytime clothes to freshen up and slip into the cotton of a light dress, pale in the evening air. Harriett and I stretched our legs, prickled by teasing blades of grass, our long locks intermingling glints of chestnut as they fanned out on the wooden floor of the porch.

I don't remember her childhood face. I suppose that's normal. There are photographs, of course, and Petite Mère's portraits. But she transformed everything, and I do hold it against her somewhat. She distorted the clear features of our youth into swirls of gouache. I simply remember the presence of other people, the warmth of the little animal that was Harriett. How full and whole I felt with her little arm brushing mine, her head leaning heavily against my shoulder. I would push her away, You're crushing my veins, I said. I can still see how she moved as a little girl, but she herself as a whole person has been replaced by the last image I have of her, that of an adult woman. I can no longer recall faces as they once were, but that has nothing to do with old age. I was already aware of this as an adolescent, and it troubled me deeply. When I was leafing through a photo album I'd noticed that Harriett no longer had her little girl face. I realized how much she'd grown without my being aware of it, since we were together all the time, and we laughed at the same things, and almost always saw the same patch of world at the same time. I would show her a lizard scurrying through the brush, and our gazes met in the verdant streak of the fleeting little reptile. I would have liked to keep her forever, that shadow which mingled constantly with my own, the hand I found spontaneously the moment I reached for it, our squabbles as sisters, as kids, too happy to have one another to appreciate it fully. We fought over nearly everything. It wasn't the same thing with the cousins or even Louisa or Klaus. They were older. They didn't even understand our games anymore, or what surprised us, at least not completely. I admired them or envied them more than anything, or I hated them because they were growing up and would eventually go away. Harriett was my anchorage in childhood, and therefore in the House. It was our beds that were side-by-side, our shutters that the daylight filtered through, our projects murmured in the hissing glow of the bedside lamp, our knowing gazes at the dinner table . . . On the other hand, I do remember her gaze, yes, perfectly. Her serious large eyes, the color of an autumn lake, with dull specks glinting deep within, like two coins buried in silt, faintly shimmering near the surface, changing with each ripple of water.

As children we never went to the lake. I think we didn't yet know it existed. One summer we found out that Klaus and Aleksander went there every morning to skip stones, and we thought it was disgraceful they'd never said anything. Here was I, who always got up so early and waited in the kitchen for the morning mist to lift, yet I'd never run into them. I felt that Klaus had betrayed me when he informed us so blithely at the breakfast table; Bertie had been entertaining us with stories about the places he'd explored in the garden as a child, and which we hadn't. "We had a secret lake," said Uncle Bertie. "Do you remember?" he said to Petit Père, who shook his head with a smile, rolling his eyes menacingly in our direction. "Where was it?" we cried, Harriett, Louisa, the cousins and I. And there it was, the scandal broke and the way we saw the garden would never be the same. "We know where it is," Aleksander said. The lake was no longer really on the property, it had been bought by the town a century earlier, so that the local fisherman could cast their lines there. To reach it from our place, you had to go under the blue curtain of the weeping willow at the edge of the orchard, all the way at the far end, then scramble through the thorny bushes, and finally jump over a fairly deep ditch where the rushes and long silvery grasses of the lake shore intertwined. The silky thickets rustled with the scrabbling of moorhens and frogs, and there were swarms of mosquitoes. After listening raptly to his description, we were stunned. It was as if we'd just discovered the ruins of a mythological temple at the end of the garden, as if suddenly a gateway to new possibilities had been opened, for new games by the water's edge, and fantastic stories to be told, with the songs of dryads and the enchantments of mermaids. "Can we go swimming there?" Magda instantly squealed. "Yes, if you're fond of eels," retorted Uncle Bertie with a ferocious expression, pinching his daughter's cheeks. "I don't care, I want to go," decreed Harriett, as indignant as I was. Petite Mère was astonished: "You never took me there," and Petit Père blushed and said, "It's just I don't really like the place." And so they told the old story, or rather Bertie told it, with relish: in that lake, when they were little, a dead body had been found. The gendarmes came to fish it out, a terrible gorgon of a woman with long watery strands wrapped all around her neck, as if the deep lake had strangled her. She'd been a neighbor, and her husband had dragged her by the hair to the lake. Petit Père seemed horrified as Bertie told the story, as if it were some sort of joke. Harriett, with her chin on her fist—I can see it so clearly—gazed fascinated at Bertie's wide red cheeks as he imitated a face disfigured by a silent scream, the face of the terrible gorgon, the drowned woman of the water lily lake.

I believe we entered adolescence quite abruptly, not long after that revelation, by way of some inexplicable temporal quirk, some footbridge between the surface of the lake and the surface of time. The fact remains that the following summer, we hardly set foot in the forest. We spent all our time by the lake. Klaus had invited strangers, friends from the Collège, he said, lanky young men with wild hair who all stood about smoking while looking inspired. Klaus stopped hiding at that point, and with his friends began smoking in front of our parents, and I was mad at them because they didn't even seem surprised. Petit Père just patted him on the shoulder, as if acknowledging his son had attained a certain maturity. "Just don't go drinking alcohol," he said, with a sidelong, knowing look at Bertie and the crimson cheeks he wore whenever he came back up from the cellar, where he'd gone to "check on the stock." We all knew that Bertie had a problem, but that was part of his role—the bon vivant, the mischief-maker, the great devourer of flesh. We let him be, and probably we shouldn't have—after all, ogres never live long. They make everyone laugh at family dinners and then they die, and it comes as no surprise, but the laughter is sorely missed.

The summer when Klaus's friends came, as I was saying—I must have been twelve or thirteen—marked our entrance into a more troubled world. For a start, the sudden appearance in our shared life, in our secret lair buried deep in the pine trees, in our family House, of a gang of youths who had shared none of our past: this changed all our relationships, in a scarcely perceptible way. There were three or four of them: I remember in particular a blond young man with short curls, Paulus, who looked like a nice boy, always ready to help, but in the depths of his eyes there was a mischievous glow which did not inspire trust. Then there was Lukas, a beanpole with hair the color of ripe straw, and a long rather pointed nose, and such class! Always with one hand in his pockets, and trousers so neat that the cousins and I wondered if he didn't iron them during the night, in secret, when everyone in the House was asleep. I've forgotten the names of the other two; one of them was a stocky, touchy, brown-haired boy, who was as fidgety as a racehorse, the other one was a very discreet redhead, his skin speckled with caramel stars. Obviously, the excitement that preceded their arrival at the House was enhanced by Klaus's promise that they were "good-looking, brilliant, and cultured." Louisa and the cousins were already swooning. They asked for descriptions, evaluations of their personality, and they immediately began making plans, squabbling over favors, virtually plotting in advance their summer romances. Magda seemed to be more accustomed to this sort of thing, goodness knows how. She must have been seeing someone during the year, and now she was feeling more womanly than ever and superior to us, with all of her sixteen years. I observed Louisa warily. I knew she had what it took to outshine her cousins. During the year she'd acquired a haughty, heady beauty, which distinguished her. Louisa had a divine nose, the envy of the entire family, short and straight, willful and noble, with no bump, or the pointed end we'd all been stuck with. Her eyes were a more luminous green than our own, and her hair was not dull like mine but a honeyed chestnut of tight curls. When she became aware she was being watched, she knew how to project a casual demeanor. Her nonchalant allure, those eyes of hers which, as she scanned the horizon, knew exactly how to catch the light and thus explode with jade and gold, were all harbingers of approaching danger by the name of Klaus's four friends. Harriett and I were still children, that is to say, still immersed in the physical ungainliness of that in-between time (although

Harriett was just as adorable that summer), and we could sense the threat reverberating like the drumming of a storm deep in the countryside, very far away, charging the air with invisible filaments of electricity. So much so that before they'd even set one loafered foot in the House, we already hated them, contrary to the rest of the House, who were putting on their finest and freshest for the arrival of these invigorating youngsters.

I remember that summer as a gleaming moiré ribbon in the bright green of the weeping willow, whose delicate leaves rippled upon the surface of the lake with each breath of air. We let ourselves drift along the grassy shore, leaving our dresses in a hollow of thick roots, and we slipped into the dull water that shivered with flashes of gold. It smelled of silt, and you couldn't enjoy more than two breast-strokes without your fingers tangling in the stems of the water lilies and the viscous filaments of the watery plants that swayed everywhere beneath our feet in the blue-green murk. Water spiders burst sporadically into ugly waltzes on the surface, and the banks, where frogs and moorhens nested, echoed at times with frightening rustling noises. We were silent in the sweltering emerald heat of the lake, we swooned in the sun as droplets of brown water trickled along our tanned arms as we dried off on the pier. Venomous, our guests buzzed with their deep, young male voices, and their gazes would linger at length on Louisa's and the cousins' pale legs. Harriett and I spied on their spying, and the tension that passed between our watchful eyes caused the heavy atmosphere of a sultry evening to hover over the entire lake. The girls vied in their ruses to attract the attention of the two more charismatic guests, Paulus and Lukas, and slowly, without saying a word, they bent over to pick up their towels, or skillfully uncoiled their water-gorged hair in the small of their backs as they made their way toward the stand of willows. The boys, enthralled, burst into nervous laughter and guiltily looked away. In the glaring sunlight of a hot afternoon, we hated them.

They were all staying in Klaus's attic, and for the occasion Aleksander, exalted by my brother's gang, had also migrated there in manly emulation. In the evening we heard them bay with laughter like hyenas. We suspected, from the effluvia of their morning breath, that there were flasks of alcohol hidden in the trunks in the attic. They spent half the night getting drunk up in the eaves of the House, and soiled the parquet floors with their dirty feet, knocking over pedestal tables as they staggered to the toilet through the silence of our sleep. The grownups said nothing, went on with their summer routine; even Aunt Hilde moderated her reproachful grey gaze so there would be no more arguments.

I was angry with Klaus all summer. By autumn, I was still angry. He didn't even notice; he no longer spent much time with us. His studies at the Conservatoire eventually won his heart, and in the warmth of the attic he was quietly becoming the best trumpet player of his generation. Sometimes in the evening as I went past my parents' bedroom I could hear worried murmuring. Klaus was more radiant than ever and, at the same time, enigmatic, living in the glow of a brilliance that completely surpassed our comprehension.

Louisa's behavior that summer disappointed me as well. It was easier for me to avoid her, as I didn't have to force my nature to spurn her. But while I didn't understand her, I also admired her a great deal—my sister, with the velvet skin that caught the honeyed daylight so well. When the long, soft tendrils of desire slid over my skin at adolescence, it was Louisa I wanted to resemble, to seduce her men, and love them.

The summer I turned fourteen, I think it was, was the first summer I felt rather fed up with being a child. In mid-July, Harriett pointed out to me that we hadn't built any cabins yet.

I was ashamed. I hadn't noticed, and what was worse, I hadn't felt the urge to build cabins. Somewhat confused, I nevertheless followed her into the woods, not to spoil her childish enthusiasm, and in hopes she might restore mine to me. She skipped among the fir trees, the way I used to in summers gone by, with the carefree buoyancy of a little fairy. Listless with the insidious heat, I was already feeling the heavy symptoms of womanhood. My sole aspiration was to stay indoors. I only half confessed to this change; I thought my health was declining, that my muscles had atrophied during the winter. I tried to explain away the phenomenon as some ordinary ailment, the strangeness or rarity of which would save me from my overwhelming shame. This shame at having changed made me act for days on end as if I were still the same, for Harriett's sake. I owed it to her. It had always been just the two of us in this world, our nimble feet on the carpet of blue pine needles, our terrors at nightfall, our dream-like murmurings in the room with the closed shutters. I thought I'd been infected with Louisa's character. Since the spring my dreams had been inhabited by handsome boys who looked a little bit like Paulus or some obscure individual in my class. In fact, the intrusion of Klaus's friends into the House had had greater impact than I'd realized—an intimate impact, belatedly. The boys' bare shoulders, the fine down on their still-young torsos, their bursts of laughter had brought with them an appetite for the other, which had now become all-consuming. I realized with horror that I could no longer be satisfied with the things that had made my childhood so vivid. I increasingly turned down Harriett's offers to play. With her big dark eyes she anxiously studied my face. The terrible disappointment I could read in her gaze was wrenching. I recognized that look we'd both reserved for Louisa last summer when she was giggling at the dinner table with Lukas, swooning with laughter in the evening air.

Not to be subjected to Harriett's gaze I avoided her. I got up long before she did and went up to the attic to read. Her little voice cried my name all morning. At lunch our shoulders no longer touched. She hardly ate, sat slumped in her chair, so, so, so disappointed.

Those were the wasted summers, between age fourteen and seventeen. I was full of spite and bitter fantasies. I envied Louisa as she casually exuded her heady scent of crushed grass. One day I snuck into her room and rummaged through her dresser. I sprayed a puff of perfume in the hollow of my wrist. But I didn't smell the same. In my flesh I bore the stigmata of a nymph, the impatience of every sylvan or lacustrine virgin. I wanted to feel the blaze of a thousand gemstones on my skin, to breathlessly inhale the jasmine of an oriental palace, to faint away in the arms of a thousand sultans and bandits.

I sought the shade of the attic room all day long, to daydream at leisure. The book slipped from my hands. I pictured mysterious strangers, whom I'd find lying on the shore of the lake in the liquid light of languorous days. I felt their lips on mine, in countless scenarios set in the House, or among the apple trees in the orchard, under the weeping willows by the lake, beneath the blue fir trees in the forest.

Petrified, I never went down to the village. Louisa was constantly away from the House; with consuming envy, I imagined her drowning her gaze in that of some handsome blond country lad. Klaus didn't bring his friends that year. I would have given anything to see Paulus again. My vague desire, without an object, had landed on him by chance, hopelessly, a fantasy reinforced by his impossible personality. I would probably never see him again, and desired him all the more desperately. I idealized him, last summer seemed so long ago. I made his jaw more square, his shoulders broader, his arms muscular and bronzed. Louisa came back in the evening. I breathed in, discreetly, as she walked by, anxiously scrutinizing her impassive, tranquil face. I was sure she'd been rolling in the hay with any old local boy; my gaze combed through her hair with the fear of finding a sprig. She always said she'd been to see her girlfriends in the village. I could have wept.

I began studying flesh. Suzy's, pink and full, so soft to Uncle Bertie's furtive touch, as he would suddenly grasp her hip along a corridor. Aleksander's slim, nervous figure, the sharp contours of his shoulders, the sun-dark veins on his forearms. Had he already been with a girl? And Klaus? Girls must have fancied them, for sure. Klaus above all. If I were a boy, would I be more handsome than him, or like him? Would I ever meet someone? In bed at night I fretted, next to Harriett who was sound asleep, exhausted by her childhood escapades. I envied her. I wished she could stay a child forever, and never know this strange disquiet I suffered.

Sweaty, sticky skin, our cousins' heavy perfumes, the wispy hairs on their damp necks: I noticed everything. One night I got up for a glass of water. I went past Suzy and Bertie's room. In the blue mugginess of the corridor I could hear dull groans and hoarse breathing, like that of a wild animal. The sound of cloth rubbing, repeatedly, obsessively, threateningly. Then nothing. Paralyzed, I didn't dare move. The stifled sounds of lips kissing eventually made me flee.

I fell into the habit of getting up every night. I would quickly go downstairs then wander around the ground floor, like a ghost of blue gauze in my nightgown. I enjoyed the solitude of those forbidden hours when everyone in the House was abandoned in their bed. Through the open windows in the kitchen the heady smell of flowers rose to my temples, and the deep violet of the warm night poured into the House. I leaned against the sink, listening to the chirring of crickets, calming my breath, taking deep lungfuls of motionless air. My gaze searched the garden as it sighed in the shadow. Perhaps a lover was waiting for me there, standing pale among the trees. I would see him, and smile, and steal quietly from the House, stepping lightly down the warm steps of the porch, and I'd run and lose myself in his arms.

There was never anyone.

The high point of this tropical fever was reached during the summer I was seventeen. After the crisis came calm. Like on the day following a heat wave, I emerged dazed and relieved.

That summer, toward the end of July, Louisa took the cousins to a village fête. For a week I'd fretted, wondering whether I should go or not. I had tried on all my dresses and didn't like any of them, and I didn't dare ask Louisa to lend me one. Everything made me look childish. I would rather stay at home than look ridiculous. All night I waited in the silence of the kitchen for them to return. At around three in the morning I heard their carefree laughter piercing the inky stillness of the sleeping trees. I hurried up to my room before they could cross the entrance hall. The next day I approached them slyly, filled with burning curiosity. They trumpeted loudly enough for all to hear, letting the boys' names slip with delight from their laughing lips. So they had met some boys. Far from my fierce wariness of four years earlier, when Klaus's friends had seemed like intruders to me, I secretly hoped they'd bring those boys here. I wanted to be besieged, like a conquered city.

During that week, Louisa and the cousins spent another evening in the village, then the following morning, from a window on the first floor, I saw a car full of young people come down the lane: boys and girls, with colorful voices, carrying baskets and balls in their arms. They went off under the trees in a decadent procession led by a simpering Louisa in a short dress of gold stripes. I suspected they were on their way to the lake. I hurried to find my swimsuit and got changed, hands trembling, checking at least four times with my palm whether my legs felt soft. Down I went, stiff with apprehension, and I made my way through the weeping willows, guided by their shouts and the sound of splashing. The way there seemed endless, and I tried to hurry, as if they were about to disappear beneath the water lilies. I tore my legs on the brambles, scratched my skin in the tall grasses that quivered with heat in the sunlight. Every second lost seemed like so many precious moments Louisa was stealing—she didn't waste a second, ablaze on the pontoon, offering her triumphant body to everyone's gaze.

At last through the rushes I could see the shining surface of the water in its emerald setting. I approached the lake where the bright young people were frolicking in the dark green water. They paused when they saw me coming. Once again I felt as if I were breaking a spell. But Louisa, with surprising warmth, took me by the arm. "My sister, Isadora." "Is she the youngest?" asked one of the boys. "No, I'm seventeen," I cried, somewhat too quickly.

I spent the afternoon with them. In their teasing presence, I regained my own girlish mischief: I was funny, witty, hardly embarrassed. They tolerated me. I joined them again the next day, and all the days that followed, making use of the friendship of a very shy boy named Randy, who was quite ordinary to look at. I only had eyes for Salem, to whom Louisa seemed very close. And then I saw him put his arm around Magda. I understood that all the girls were in love with him, and that this merry company was merely an act, disguising the group's true interest: Salem.

I never managed so much as a few words with him. I was invisible. I let Randy kiss me at the end of the summer. He was a bit silly but, surprisingly good at kissing. It was my first kiss, in the soft blue light of late afternoon by the lake, behind the rushes. Nothing else happened and, by autumn, I'd stopped thinking about boys. I'd got what I wanted.

I haven't kissed anyone in so long. I will die soon, and my lips will remain virginal in their fresh grave. So long ago now, all the kisses I gave: mischievous kisses, biting, tingling the nerves and pricking the heart; sleepy kisses, languid in the gloom of a closed room; kisses of reunion, cool and troubled by the fear of no longer quite recognizing each other. Some people kiss the same lips their whole life long and then, in the end, kiss them no more. Familiar lips are like pieces of furniture you no longer notice, I suppose. They disappear until you notice them again.

I will kiss no more, now, there will be no more tight embraces, breath mingling rhythmically, the kiss intensifying in a single, joint urge, the plunge into clear waters; beneath the warm sand, flesh. How serene we become when the years of love are over.

From that moment on, after the kiss, summer became for me a season of placid truce. All the emotion of the spring was blurred by the crushing heat at the edge of the woods; I grew calm. I stayed with my family, got used once again to their particular preoccupations, their morning faces, their hoarse evening voices. I rediscovered myself in them and in the cool walls of the House. I patiently gathered the pieces of myself that I'd mislaid during the academic year, I returned to my reading by the window, and to my inconsequential daydreaming.

I became a child again, in summer. It was a time for regression when, far from the city and my friends at the Collège, I re-immersed myself in childhood sensations: licking the sun on my own skin, dipping into the cool lake water, closing my eyes to listen to the birdsong, afternoon naps in a cradle of leaves. The summers of my twenties were peaceful. I hurried about, helping in the garden or with the laundry, and I replaced my erstwhile adventurous outings with other more humdrum quests, but that gave me the same freedom. I hung the big cool sheets to dry, humming to myself, and as the laundry line bisected the sun, it seemed to form the likeness of an ancient shield, its edges pricked with arrows. I took pleasure in dreaming, I ambled everywhere more peacefully, without being startled, without laughing. I remained astonished and silent before the spectacle of the dawn, the sight of insects with their iridescent carapace filing slowly along the porch, or the rather scary dragonflies perched on the pontoon by the lake. I didn't drive them away anymore. I was alone and calm. I went on ever longer walks, going farther than before, through the woods with their rays of enchanted light, beneath the foliage where specks of sifted sunlight danced. Wearing a long linen dress that billowed against my calves, I strode across the silent clearings, with their sunken-city charm. I would come out onto a flaxen meadow where stalks swayed lazily. I hummed without humming, I murmured invented dialogues to myself alone, and broke off when a lizard scurried suddenly through a hollow in the undergrowth. Silence and song, that was what the world was made of in summer: the insolent silence of a cloudless sky, the song of the warm breeze curling around one's ears, unhurried birds and the tangle of tall grass. Sometimes a trickle of brown water flowed along the bottom of a coppery ditch. A frog was croaking there—I crouched down to see it better. It always took my eyes a certain amount of time to adjust to the earth's uniformly powdery tones, and at last in a viscous throbbing I could discern the little amphibian's fluttering heart beat. A strange pride came over me at that point, a reminiscence of childhood conquests, of the astonished discoveries my cousins and I made all over the garden. Now I enjoyed it alone, the glory of penetrating nature's secret, of encountering one of its unobtrusive creatures.

I missed having a companion. Very early on, at around seventeen, Harriett began to use her summers to explore the world.

We never knew when she would be home. She'd taken our adventurous enterprise to new heights, and filled her notebooks with sketches of foliage larger and bluer than our own. The garden no longer satisfied her. Before long she came to the House for only one month, generally August, arriving to great fanfare, her skin tanned by more humid suns. And then, of course, she went away again, leaving me perpetually on my own.

As for the others, it was as I expected. Louisa spent her summers with this or that lover, this or that girlfriend, in various country houses, in seaside resorts glittering like giant conch shells washed ashore at sunset. She called us on the phone, and in the background were the sounds of cafés or jazz. We could barely understand what she was saying, but she laughed and told us everything was fine.

Klaus toured in the summer with the conservatory orchestra. He played evenings in noisy towns where he was adored, and his voice grew husky with girls and cocktails.

Hilde, Aleksander, the cousins, and even Uncle Bertie eventually stopped coming as well. The drive was long and had become increasingly difficult, because of gridlock, and tar melting in the heat, and Suzy said her legs felt heavy. They would stay for only two weeks, to make the most of the fresh air and tranquility, but they soon grew bored. Something had been broken.

I was almost thirty. My summers were being depleted of their wonders. The House, with its veneer of white wood, began to reverberate with ever more unbearable waves of heat. That heavy, electric sky, which I hardly noticed as a child, or which, at least, did not keep me from roaming freely, now weighed on my shoulders with its liquid cape of yellow, a mantle drenched in burning poison, the bite of the sun on my skin. I began to adopt the doleful moaning that used to so exasperate me when the grownups would drift around the House all day long like sleeping elephants. I gradually understood, or at least my drowsy flesh made me understand, why the grownups wouldn't play with us in the summer. I became slow, as they had done. My torso and hips, grown heavy, my thickened thighs all constituted that much extra weight on my tall skeleton, pressing me into the ground, anchoring me in the earth. No more could I run eternally breathless beneath the low-lying branches of the fir trees. On entering the water I was heavy, dulled by the heat, hypnotized by the cool ripples of the lake, and all I sought was the close, wanton embrace of its cold arms. No more gilt sequins sliding over the surface of the water, just blades of light in my eyes slicing into my brain like an ant building its palace. I no longer observed, I closed my eyes, drifted slowly on the water, while the pink warmth of my eyelids throbbed gently. Everything was dazzling, exhausting. Skin damp, only slightly refreshed, I went back under the willows, reached silently for my things, and returned to the House to collapse onto my light little childhood bed. By the first days of July I was already weary of summer. I could no longer imagine myself as queen or naiad, the support of the world had fallen silent, the heat annihilated everything. The garden was crushed with sunlight, ironed flat by the relentless yellow reverberation.

Petite Mère's summer migraines became more and more violent after she turned fifty. We weren't to make any noise, but proceed on tiptoe past the darkened salon, where we could just make out the pale, inert form on the sofa, her arms twisted in pain. When I brought her something hot to drink, the sound of the spoon against the glass caused her to give a terrible moan. She was no longer my mother, sweet and inspired, but a poor weak wretch, the folds of her gauzy dressing gown creased with the tension of her fingers. She murmured words without letters. Before long she needed stronger medication. Petit Père went to the village pharmacy to fetch an entire arsenal of potions that had to be mixed, dosed, and sweetened with sugar. That is when I became a shaman again. Between her lips I inserted the liqueur of death, of the sleep of the senses, deceitful narcotic as nectar. Petit Père would sigh and moan, then disappear for long hours at a stretch. I knew that he loved my mother, and to see her like that drove him insane with worry. I felt a certain scorn toward him; I couldn't stand his helpless tears. Both of them were poisoning the House with their troubled breath.

I suggested she be taken to the hospital, or to a rest home, where the peace and fresh air might reinvigorate her. She was duly moved. Her condition worsened, but at least the House revived. I flung wide the windows of the veranda, letting the glorious daylight splash into the salon, chasing the shadows, and the warm air effaced the lingering odor of suffering.

Petite Mère's illness filled me with unease. I vaguely sensed that she wouldn't be cured. Petit Père alone had not yet grasped this, he insisted on going to see her, and always came home even more downcast and dazed, his cheeks hollow. You're wearing yourself out, Petit Père; you're watching her decline with a hopefulness that does not serve her well.

I was reproached for not going to see her often enough. The terrible accusation leveled at me was that I preferred the four walls of the House. Everyone called Petit Père in the evening to inquire how she was doing. He would tell them about his visits in a weary voice, and I discreetly left the room. I wasn't interested. It wasn't my Petite Mère, in that place, groaning in a dead room. For me, Petite Mère was out on the veranda, translucent, she was painting invisible canvases that we didn't know how to see. She filled my memories, her arms scented with flowers, she smiled at me in my sleep, she permeated everything. Staying in the House meant staying by her, the real her, but of course no one else saw it that way. Louisa came to spend the summer at the House with her husband and her little boy. She rushed around, went twice a day to the clinic, drove Petit Père, chose his shirts for him, felt sorry for him, spoiled him. I avoided her all summer. I avoided her gaze that overwhelmed me with a lack of understanding and a surfeit of reproach. On the morning of the funeral she grasped my arm in the corridor and stared at me, her eyes shining with tears. We didn't understand one another. We had never understood one another, and that was something that, perhaps, I had always known.

Then the wind blows past, sweeps away the ashes.

At last we began to speak of the real Petite Mère again, not the sick one, but the living one from the past. They reproduced her funny faces, with tender eyes and joyful words. Ah! The truth is that I hadn't waited until her death to remember her. The past has always been easier for me than for them. They live too much in the sorrow of the present.

I had realized that the past was the only thing that made my life worth living. The House, our memories, and I: we would do great things together. Because familiar things will never die.

Now someone had to do the canning. The herbaria in my room made them conclude I knew more about plants than anyone else. I was charged with making the jam, and with this tenderly imperious decision, I sensed I had become the new mistress of the House. This minute task, once Petite Mère's chore, of filling glass prisms with the sticky mellifluence of stewed fruit, now fell to me as naturally as the transfer of power from king to son. Sealing the lids over the dormant treasures of our family land was a materialization of the link between the sacrifice of looking after the orchard and the future pleasure of an entire year of delicious tartines. The sacrifice and the reward, all the tiresome mornings spent weeding, repainting the House, mowing the lawn, replenishing the woodpile, cleaning all three floors: it was all consecrated at the end of every summer by the dozen or so jars of jam standing in a row on the bottom shelf in the cellar. It was the justification of all our efforts, of everything the House required of us. "Oh, how good it feels to be out in the country, after all, with our own garden." And at breakfast they let out unconsciously overacted exclamations of joy, followed by appreciative little comments, almost to themselves: "It's better than last year's," "You can really taste the fruit," "Is it strawberry or raspberry?"

It was never-ending. Now, when I think back on those years, I am filled with dejection. I rushed about, from cellar to attic. Petit Père was good for nothing now, the poor man, his limbs were weak, and the realization he was in his sixties was a heavy blow to him. Petite Mère's death had affected all of us differently. It had reminded the older members of the family of their own approaching death, and made the others aware that soon they would have to look after the House.

I was clearly cut out for the job. I knew very well that one day I alone would hold the long gold keys, with their strange embellishments. I had fantasies of myself as head of the clan, an austere matron in a tweed dress, sinister and content in the solitude of her Manor House. I wished for just such a situation, saw in it all the charm of a delightful hermitage, and I was almost looking forward to the future disappearance of the heads of the family—Petit Père, Hilde, and Bertie—so that I could be alone at last to wander solemnly through the corridors, with the weight of the dead on my shoulders.

I wanted to prove to the family that I could manage, that because I loved it so much, the House would be gentle with me, conciliatory, that it would delay the decay of the roof, the peeling of the paint, and would stay warm and comfortable for the rest of my days.

The first summers of my solitude were exquisite, full of the lingering grace of new light. Life in the House was finally being lived at my rhythm. I found an excellent pretext to lure the

Aberfletches back to the House. I called them on the phone at the end of June, and told them how precious their help would be to me to paint the façade this year, or to pick the fruit, just a little help and nothing more, and then there'd be the tranquility of the sunlit woods and the cool turquoise waters of the lake. They yielded to my pleas. I leapt for joy, opened the windows wide, and let my song mingle with that of the little forest creatures that swarmed with impatience. I whirled here and there, as in childhood, in the dazzling hallway with its faded paint of blue foliage. I waxed the banister of the staircase, got out the soup tureens, made up the beds in our former bedrooms. The cousins', Louisa's, Klaus's garret. Everything smelled of clean linen, and the white walls beamed, as if laughing.

They arrived at the beginning of July. Their shiny latest-model cars, straight from that modern City life that I didn't envy in the least, drove with a crunching of tires up the lane that led to the entrance, and I ran down to greet them. For one second I was inside and they were out, I could see them through the doorway, the sweetest sight on earth. It used to be our place, and now they were coming to my place, at my invitation, and it was through me alone that they were permitted to enter the world where we used to be *enfants terribles*. They came through the door, hugging me joyfully, laden every year with women, spouses, and children. In the silence of my moist eyes I crowned them kings again as I watched them excitedly climbing our staircase to re-take possession of their realm.

I followed slowly behind them, in the certainty of my empire, because I knew that while nothing had changed, everything was suffused with my perfume and my voice. The House belonged to me, and I belonged to it. On taking possession of the keys I had saturated the walls with my shadow. The familiar strangers who had come back, therefore, were entering my heart and setting their opened suitcases in my veins; perhaps without knowing it.

With an indulgent smile I let them rediscover the place. I understood their wonder, and it truly made me happy. They shared my domain and appreciated it almost as much as I did, in those moments of arrival. They asked countless questions, the children were already running up and down the corridors as if it were conquered territory, between our too-heavy adult legs. And each of those adults pestered me with the same question, which they asked once, then kept silent. "Oh, you're still sleeping in that room and that little bed?" I quickly closed the door. They mustn't speak of my little sister as if she were a thing of the past, as if she were a room one could move out of. It would have been unthinkable for me to leave that room with its twin beds. It would have been unthinkable to part with a single toy chest, a single stuffed animal that Harriett had pressed against her heart as she drifted deep into the sleep of a six-year-old. Or the bedside lamp that I'd always switched off too late to her liking. To change my bedroom would mean leaving Harriett to sleep all alone, and to fear that she might awake in the middle of the night and find my bed empty, then search the shadows with her big, puzzled eyes.

They looked at me rather pityingly, in the silence that followed their remark. Then I replied, saying simply, "Oh, I'm just so used to my bed." They breathed out, as if relieved by the rational explanation of a natural phenomenon. They generally left me alone with Harriett's memory for the entire summer. They knew I was the one who had suffered most from her death, which still felt so raw.

As I observed Klaus, Louisa and her husband—Gallead it was at the time, Aleksander and his wife Pelen and their children Mellie and Conrad, with little Kurt, all enjoying their summer at the House, it seemed to me that we might start again as a family, weave memories for these children as luminous as our own. The cousins never came. They stayed at home with their respective husbands and children, cooking turkey in the oven even during heat waves.

I looked at my niece and nephews, tiny and shrill, galloping across the garden, and I envied them, oh how I envied them . . . Mellie was a tall blond child with wise eyes that overflowed with metallic water the way Aleksander's did. She protected the two younger children and had them running from the end of her hand as if it were an organic leash. This small chain of children was wound and unwound as they ran through the forest, preceded by the ringing of their rascally laughter. They returned from the woods in the evening, worn out, and could not stop talking, endlessly rhapsodizing about their cabins; their parents gushed with delight, but I sat solemnly on my chair, glancing out of the corner of my eye at the twigs caught in their fine hair. They had stolen my woods, pillaged my forest with their little paws, disfigured it with their hideous cabins, and here they thought they were the first! First and only, their primitive step upon the promised land, the explorers of Atlantis, the inventors of formidable cities? And they were praised, my brother took them on his lap and planted loud kisses on their cheeks, Louisa was amazed at the dexterity of her little Kurt, Aleksander and Pelen exchanged a gaze stunned with self-satisfied parenthood. But had they all really forgotten our palaces burrowed among the branches? Our private wars, our opposing sides, our strategies and afternoons spent dragging heavy ropes and sheets to rig the sails of our vessels? Did they not remember anything? Did becoming an adult mean having to forget how ingenious we were as children, and wonder instead at the pale exploits of offspring who've invented nothing? I scowled, and went to fetch the cheese platter from the kitchen. And their strident voices, squealing *and then I and then I* all through the meal; so, had we really been such unbearable children? Little princes all bloated with conquest and scorn for the grownups too heavy to follow us up to our perches? I suppose we had.

They came five summers in a row. I no longer needed to call them in June to find out whether they were coming or not. It was taken for granted, they opened the door all by themselves. What had initially seemed like a temporary sharing of my kingdom eventually began to feel like a disloyal siege. They arrived with bigger and bigger suitcases, to stay longer and longer. The children were growing, their parents were becoming bloated, and I found the sudden shattering of my solitude impossible to bear; not knowing what they were up to, I couldn't stand hearing their nocturnal sorties or the untimely flush of the toilet in the silence of each floor; could not stand their muddy shoes in the entrance hall. They looked on me as a childless, and clueless, old maid. They probably thought that I'd never slept with anyone, right, and that my body was made of ice and my womb was barren. No one bothered Klaus about his celibacy. He merely gave a wink when anyone asked him about his bachelor life in the City. A girl in every concert hall, of course; he implied that there was a parade to and from his bed of all the pretty young music lovers in the land. "Musicians have an irresistible charm," my big brother said, and I didn't laugh. And this absence of laughter, yet again, against my will, signaled that I was that despised archetype; I would have so liked for all of them, with their families, to envy me for once, for my solitude and freedom. Klaus was not even interested in my life, I was perfectly aware of that, he probably thought I had nothing to tell, cloistered all year round in the House. He must have thought that I'd become dull and boring now, that I didn't read anymore, that there was nothing in my countrydweller's mind beyond the next crop of zucchini in the garden. He surely thought that none of his friends would ever fancy his little sister Isadora, now. As the years passed he must have found me uglier and uglier, but he never told me, I could see it in his rather proud gaze whenever he held Louisa against his shoulder—Louisa who was always fresh and smartly turned out, even when things were not going well with her husband.

The children had become irksome. Barbarian. Their bodies had expanded, and this eliminated the rather sweet disproportion little children have, their big heads, startled gazes. Now they looked like imperious little adults, full of demands, lassitude, trouble, and squabbles with their parents. They spent more and more time in the attic, opening the chests, even though I'd told them not to. I heard them carelessly dragging the trunks under the eaves, producing terrible scraping noises of metal and wood.

Then came the famous breaking point. The children's parents and I were vaguely reading in the salon, and I'd been mutely listening to the shameless commotion above our heads. There was a terrible racket, with dull thuds and cruel laughter, the sharp cries of childish brats. Sitting tensely, deep in my armchair, I studied the impassive faces of my peers. They did not seem to have noticed the massacre unfolding overhead. I let out a sigh, wriggled in my chair, nothing worked. So it would have to be sorted between myself and the usurpers. I put my book on the side table and slowly got up, one hand gripping the folds of my linen dress. I went past the sofas, the others didn't budge. I felt a nervous excitement rising inside me as I walked lightly across the hall and started up the winding levels of the spiral staircase. I knew these silent steps. I reached the door to the attic, as discreet as a fox. I yanked the door open. My gaze is suddenly lost in the gloom, just in time to see Conrad—Aleksander and Pelen's little redhead—waving his fist triumphantly under his sister's nose, tightly clenched around Harriett's wooden fairy, the precious little fairy she used to take everywhere until she tired of it. A vision of horror, a chiaroscuro tableau of infamy, the plump arm I'm seizing forcefully, there are tears, my hand sweeping through the air straight at a cheek, furious screams, my brother tearing us apart, the children and I in a frenzy as we're hauled out of the attic. In the white corridor, a silence filled with gasps for breath. I'm holding the doll in my hand. Conrad is sobbing, snot running from his nose. Everyone is looking at me, mouths agape. Disappointed. Indignant. Horrified. My murmur pierces the silence. "Don't you dare touch Harriett's things."

They left that very evening, and never came back to spend their summer at the House.

Over the years, their stubborn silence made it clear that there was something wrong with me. That I had ruined the Aberfletch family by clinging to ghosts. That I had driven them from the House. Frankly, given the little they did for it, I wonder who did more to destroy our memories. I do wonder.

To see those brats running where we had run, to see them pillaging the dead wood of our old cabins in order to build new ones, to see them acting like kings the way we ourselves had done, it had all been unbearable to me. They knew nothing about the incandescent happiness that all of us—Harriett, Louisa, Klaus, Aleksander, Amelia, Magda and I—had known in the cool blue fir trees, on the golden lawn where clumsy moths danced in the trembling beam of the flashlight wedged between two trunks in the attic, during our summertime wakes. The sound of crickets piercing our games of hide-and-seek, hearts racing in the dry heat, embers of fear in our bellies swollen with a good lunch. Afternoon naps in the white bedrooms stitched with soft light. The fatigue in our bronzed legs, hair wild against our nape, Harriett's little hand in mine. They would never know, those bothersome brats, how happy we had been, and how much their joy had broken my heart, reviving the inaccessibility of our games. Our childhood was like an old book where the ink had faded over time, and I could not reread it when I looked at the garden spreading, virtually unchanged, into the burning dust of August days. They stole my forest, and my House with its white wooden façade that always needed painting. They stole my childhood summers, the only ones that are worth living for.

The end of summer. The end of my eyes squinting, dazzled with yellow. The end of the glass of water hurriedly filled in the kitchen, in the middle of a game, because we'd inhaled too much wind while running, and it made us thirsty. The end of raspberries nibbled from the palm of the hand, of seeds stuck in our teeth. The end of the liquid, luminous hours, of the noble immortality of holidays, the end of pine needles catching between our damp toes.

Come every first of September, mourning a world.

Autumn

The House was emptying out, like an ebbing sea, and the intangible light of the closing days of summer lingered on the surface of faces, furniture, parquet floors. What left a faint mark, like the delicate foam sighing into the sleeping sand, was the summer that had just receded. Everyone had left. Aunt Hilde and Aleksander returned to the City, Uncle Bertie retreated with all his crew to the sweet hills of the South.

Silence . . . A strong wind whirling the dry leaves, and banging the shutters on some desolate façade. The unquiet murmur of the dark firs, the woods I didn't dare visit without my cousins, for fear of spoiling the magic of the sanctuary, of finding the cabins void of meaning, hanging from dead branches.

For a few autumns there were only six of us living there, until Great-Aunt Babel's health obliged her to come back to the House for the cold season. Those autumns when we were just the six of us were the most troubling of my existence, because we weren't used to such a small circle anymore. In the constant ferment of the House and its temporary visitors, my parents played a very distant role; we had almost total freedom, and we entrusted ourselves to Klaus and Louisa's kindly supervision. When we ran into Petite Mère with her brushes, carrying a laundry basket or a garland of flowers, we were no more curious about where she was headed than she was about us. We coexisted with the grownups, dispatched our meals in no time, and only for a short spell after supper did we sit in the salon with Petit Père. It was strange. Our family unit seemed uneven, just the six of us; our equilibrium had atrophied, as if we constantly needed a more distant relative to bind us all together, to give us a convergent center of interest. We had spent the summer in the flurry and joy of being reunited with our extended family, so this sudden solitude weighed all the heavier.

Every autumn I got the impression that the House was dying, that it was drying up like the forest around us losing its tender leaves, its verdant brilliance. Before long the rains began to stain the wooden façade we'd repainted during the summer. We stayed shut indoors, school had started and took me away from the House, tore me from its kindly walls. I envied Petite Mère, who could stay calmly on the veranda, painting the orchard dripping with rain, while the wind raged outside and caused the flames in the hearth to flicker.

I didn't like school. I was bored. I was separated from my brother and sisters, even if at every recess I did see Harriett in the schoolyard, where we could play the games we would have played at the House. I always felt inadequate, incomplete, away from the House. As if a part of me were embedded in its walls. I was constantly projecting myself back there, the moment I imagined something or thought of the summer gone by. My dreams were the color of the sunlit mahogany floorboards. I'd already sensed that my brother and sisters' view of life was vastly different from mine, when I saw how they grew feverish with excitement at the prospect of returning to school. Klaus more than anyone, the brilliant student with loads of friends, his hearty laughter, his proud shoulders; he entered autumn the way an army sure of victory marches into a City. Every year, Klaus besieged his class, stole hearts, fascinated teachers, came home in the evening with his excellent report cards. Louisa applied herself, but was better at making friends than studying; she was good at art, and had a melodious voice when it came to reciting, and her hair shone in the sun as she flitted around the schoolyard—she was well-liked. Harriett, like Klaus, was brilliant, but too shy. She had not learned how to combine her rational skills with an intelligence at reading souls. And besides, she was too picky when it came to her subjects. She excelled in science, but didn't have much imagination, whereas Klaus was good at everything, without even trying. I immediately understood that he wouldn't stay here. That he'd leave for the City, to shine, because at the House, we couldn't shine. We couldn't force the wooden walls to expand for our luminous wings, so we had to fold them, and let the light glow dimly within us. That was something Klaus would never have been able to do.

At the beginning of autumn, because the cold wind slipped all too easily under the eaves, and it was freezing in the attic, Klaus slept in Louisa's room until the heat was turned on. It was always an event when our parents declared, usually on a misty Sunday morning while gazing out through the fogged-up windows, that it was beginning to feel "bitterly cold out there, the geese'll be heading south again." Because of this expression of his, and because of the feathers in Great-Aunt Babel's hat, I always imagined that something volatile flowed in her veins, and like the geese she did indeed migrate to a warmer place every winter. She left the City (to which she had returned after her summer stay at the spa) in early October, spent a weekend here, and then continued south.

The first fire of the year in the hearth was always a magnificent event. The logs, still dry from their time in the shed, seemed to give off that heady smell of summer, crackling more intensely than ever in the blackened hearth, decorated deep inside with mysterious figures of centaurs and nymphs. The heat from a radiator can in no way compare to that of a fire; that is why, toward the end, I no longer turned them on, and asked only for the fire in the salon to be lit, nothing more. The people who were looking after me knew that in any case I didn't have the money it would take to keep the House heated like in the old days—I could just imagine them murmuring behind the door, "When will she be going to a retirement home?" I really didn't care, because then I held my hands out to feel the flames licking so near, and my fingers blurred into that translucent reddish glow. The prominent veins seemed to melt back into my skin and, as my hands stood out darkly against the impetuous fire, they became a child's hands, my hands held out in the same way to enjoy some of the heat . . . to have that soft wave of molten gold flow through my blood, to feel my limbs tingling with a surge of life. I stayed there staring at the dancing flames, glued to the hearth for fear that a single step outside its glow would chill my blood forever.

There were evenings when we would leaf through the album with Petit Père. We all huddled around him on the sofa, we could only ever see bits of the photos, depending on the spot we'd managed to grab, and Louisa's hair always fell on the page when she leaned forward to see the glossy faces more closely; we would give her a hard shove, shrieking that she was being selfish, as usual. The album consisted of three or four enormous leather-bound volumes in varying shades of brown and red. The pages crackled, just like the fire; the springs in the sofa moaned when we all sat there. I have brought these volumes to my room here, because when I ask a nurse to bring me one, and he places it on my lap, the weight of it reassures and comforts me. I open the album, and the first breath that emerges is the sighing of time, a whiff of tarnished smells that immerses me once again into my home, surreptitiously, for a fraction of a second before it dissipates. I turn the pages and it's as if I can see our fingers jabbing feverishly at photographs: "Hey, that looks like Babel, with no wrinkles," "Was that her, Petit Père? Was it?," "Wow, she was so pretty," "What a change," "And where are you, huh, show us." I've forgotten a lot of the names he used to reel off, especially at the beginning of the first volume, where people I never knew, from my great-grandfather's time, were posing. I think I actually never liked these albums all that much. It annoyed me to see pictures of people I didn't know wandering around the House, acting as if they owned the place, sprawling on the sofas, laughing in the orchard, leaning their elbows on the roof of an old car parked triumphantly in the lane. The dead have no humility, there they pose, frozen forever on glossy paper, forever at home in the places where they've lived. I'm fearful of disturbing them, I refuse to throw out the dinner service that had belonged to old Léoagathe, because she loved it so much, that holy woman; and yet that dinner service annoys everyone, and it's chipped and tacky, but no one says that, because old Léoagathe, whose bones are lying crammed into the village cemetery somewhere, eaten by vermin, was first and foremost "a holy woman." What I hated more than anything were the photographs where you could see other children building cabins in the woods the way we used to, cabins that have disappeared, swallowed by the resin-laden wind, and their laughter has faded into the bark of the trees. These children were Uncle Bertie and Petit Père, with Hilde, who looked like a boy with her short hair. They were posing with their cousins—whom we never saw anymore—on the porch. The entire House was a particular color, the faded yellowish tones of old photographs; I hardly recognized it, it was the House and at the same time it wasn't. Everything looked newer, too: on some of the pictures the veranda had not even extended its glass panels at the rear of the House. Two or three photos in the first album showed smiling people posing with hammer in hand, assembling the veranda. It was strange to think that the House, like a wooden toy you can take apart, had been extended and altered, constructed, re-imagined. And for an instant the House ceased to be that immutable entity that seemed to have always been there, and must always stay there; it acquired a notion of temporality, and that was something uncomfortable. I didn't like looking at those photos, they reminded me that I too was changing, getting older from one year to the next, and that one day I would go away to study in the City, like all the others, that I would leave this world that meant everything to me—the plush lawn, the walls of white wood, the elaborate gables, and the tall dark trees.

In autumn, I also hated to see the trees losing their leaves. Fortunately there were the fir trees, standing guard, straight and proud in their elegant cloak of dark green, the last guardians of our vagabonding. Escapades into the autumn forest lacked the spice of summer. The density of humid air, the layer of heavy earth beneath our feet, still dark with the night's rainfall, made everything heavier, oppressive. The tall trees seemed more threatening, and the heady effluvia of sodden mushrooms and moss made it almost difficult to breathe when you were among the trees. The branches intertwined above our heads dripped slowly, placing the liquid tips of their invisible fingers on our hair, beading it with rain. Even running was impossible; the lawn was slippery, the humus spongy, and it sucked the soles of our feet toward the depths of the earth; we had to get out of there and run away, fast, as fast as we could, back to the House because, on top of it all, our noses were freezing and we had no handkerchiefs. We used the front door to go in, not the veranda, because we had to wipe our shoes and leave them in the entrance hall, and then we realized that our socks, too, were soaked through, and our feet were like ice. The air in the House slowly warmed us again, and Petit Père's jazz in the salon, the kettle whistling in the kitchen for Petite Mère's tea, then Louisa's mystical humming, which seemed to glide all the way down the banister, all immediately reassured us, and convinced us, for a time, to stay forever in the warm.

Louisa no longer went out into the garden once summer was over; she didn't even try. And yet I remember one occasion when she helped us to track down a hedgehog that seemed injured.

Squat and spiny like a pine cone, he'd gotten lost among the red leaves. He was like a little bear, sniffing out the fish in a river of copper, and the little gilded cockroaches wriggled past our fingers like trout. His belly throbbed like a pounding heart hidden under his skin, and Louisa was deeply moved by the prickly, gentle little creature. She picked him up and carried him quickly to a spot in the forest that was more open and where he could make his way more easily. I remember marching behind her, picturing us as knights of the forest, escorting tearful creatures toward softer carpets of moss. I loved that image of Louisa. It doesn't come to mind often—it gets buried in all the rest, engulfed by our constant arguments, devoured by her barbed comments, her arrogance, her whims, her lack of interest in the things that I loved. Louisa is acidic, like cider, bad cider. My greatest fits of rage, as a child, an adolescent, and an adult, were directed at her, brought on by her, aggravated by her offhand manner. She didn't get as annoyed as she used to, but she was more hurtful; I could have banged myself against the walls and pierced her skin with my teeth until it bled, so greatly did she prey on my nerves. And yet I liked knowing she was in the House. When she stopped coming so often, there were times when I wept with frustration. Is that the way a big sister is supposed to behave? I felt abandoned almost all the time by my older siblings, and I would have died of shame if I thought Harriett had felt that way, too. I wanted to be the best big sister possible, so that Harriett would stay with me, for a long time.

Harriett is blurry in autumn. The dead leaves are to blame, they make memories slippery.

And yet Harriett loved the autumn. She sometimes snuck out into the garden all by herself and came back saying, in a mysterious tone that annoyed me, that she'd been talking to the squirrels, and they'd listened, perched on a branch. I hated these tall tales, it was as if she was excluding me from a certain intimacy with the woods, my woods, my beloved woods, that I alone loved the way they were meant to be loved; I alone observed the trees so closely that I knew how to read the meandering of the bark. She swore it was true, that the squirrels listened, that they understood her, and everyone else laughed a little, mussing her hair, and I felt hurt. She was mine, and the woods were, too, and those two entities could not communicate without me. I was the link, still am the link, between Harriett's smile, which we have all forgotten, and the tall fir trees that I'll never see again. When they open the window in my old woman's care home room to let in some good clean air, I listen to the wild wind coming from deep in the world, and I imagine that it has blown through my forest, caressed the contours of the House, charged its gusts with the smells of resin I know so well, and my nostrils quiver with delight, until the nurse pulls me back from the window, telling me I'll catch my death. But I am dying. It fills me with rage to be here; as for Harriett, she's very lucky, she's still there, in the House, in the woods, in our little room, everywhere. I know she strolls around, letting her hand of ice trail along the cold radiators.

She calls out to me, she's waiting for me.

I don't know if I can find my way back to the House. I'm afraid the limbo where I'm meant to stay is not to be found there.

I didn't want to leave, it wasn't a choice, it never was. Departures are terrible; why do others find them so simple? Klaus and Louisa never seem to have trouble leaving; on the contrary, they have a ready suitcase and an easy road. They come and go without sorrow, the House is always open to them and always gentle, never violent, unlike the immoderate love

I feel for it and which drives me insane, when I'm away from the House, like a jealous lover. I'm glad I have only ever had one home of my own. It seems to me that to have one home after another makes a person more inconstant. Their notion of a home of one's own has been cheapened, because they've left bits of themselves in all those homes they've left behind. Klaus had several apartments, his student room in the City, dozens of hotel rooms for his concerts, beds for the night, parquet floors with knots in the wood he barely had time to notice. You spend less time thinking about the places you leave often, no doubt because you force yourself to keep from getting attached, as if to mitigate the pain that comes with being forced to move. Moving House destroys some part of us. You leave bits of yourself pinned to the wall everywhere you go, and so you are torn to pieces when you must leave. My brother disintegrated over time; no doubt it's for that reason that he is happy nowhere.

I've never cried harder than when I had to start school at the Collège in the City. Already at the end of summer I was overcome with irrational sorrow. I felt as if I'd be leaving the House forever, and Louisa sat on my bed and took me in her arms and said, You'll see, boarding school is great, you'll have loads of friends, the way I do, and the boys are cute and they laugh loudly when they walk down the hall so that you'll look out the door. But I don't want to go there, Louisa, I want to be like Harriett and stay in the House, it's not fair. Yes but Harriett is still in primary school, you know that, her turn will come, and she'll have to leave, too, and besides, you'll come back every weekend, we'll take the train together right after my last class at four o'clock. And Harriett would shoot me a petrified look from under her duvet, a look of both fascination and terror, because her big sister was going to go to the City and out into the world away from the House. I would gladly have swapped places with her.

The ride home on the weekends in that cold train was awful; it wound its way through the russet forests for forty-five minutes until it spat us out onto the platform in the village with its rain-drenched, melancholy brick houses. Petit Père was there waiting for us, and each time he looked a little thinner; I didn't know why. It was as if our absence was eroding him, and he was being pared away like a wooden statuette under the blade of a knife. We went up the winding road that led to the House and I was furious to see that I'd missed the falling of the leaves, because the branches always shed their leaves all at once, during one of the weeks I was at the Collège. Harriett ran to greet us as soon as we set foot in the entrance hall, her little laugh spiraling down the staircase, her arms enfolding us, and she smelled of the House even more than the House itself did. Her hair gave off the scent of the warm, spicy dust of old wood, richly laden with heavy odors by the rain. I held back my tears as I looked around the House and wiped my feet like a stranger, handing my coat to Petite Mère instead of tossing it joyfully onto the polished banister of the spiral staircase. I wondered how Louisa managed to deal with this feeling of estrangement, this peculiar sensation that meant we no longer felt at home anywhere; the student's sickness. Maybe it was all in my head, after all, and I was no stranger to anyone here, but I felt a physical discomfort as I opened the door to our room and saw my bed still perfectly neat the way Petite Mère had made it, with a slightly stuffy smell and the cold flat sheets of a bed that is no longer occupied. I sometimes got the impression, when I put my little suitcase at the foot of the bed, that I had died and come to haunt this place, that I was the only one who could perceive my presence in the room. I thought that if Harriett came in she would walk straight through me, as if I were invisible, intangible, and in the end, nonexistent. I was outside my body and I could smell the House, when before, it used to permeate my skin and my daily life so deeply that I hardly noticed it. On Friday evenings I felt lost, then on Saturday when I opened my eyes in my little bed and Harriett's faintly hoarse breathing creased the silence, I was as if re-integrated within the walls. And I forgot my uprooting. A new weekend at the House had begun.

I enjoyed the House even more, as if I were rediscovering it. The House gave off that flowery, spicy essence of the women in the family; Petit Père left no mark. Klaus only came back for holidays, he was a student at the Conservatoire in an even bigger town now. I didn't venture up to the attic when he wasn't there. I would have felt as if I were going into a strange dwelling walled in by adolescent secrets. I went into the cool woods very early, without Harriett, and walked cautiously among the dark, mossy trees, not to arouse the spirits of the forest. In autumn the forest became heavy, mystical. I wouldn't have felt like running there. I let the liquid chill enter into me and slowly anesthetize me, let myself go to the torpid embrace of the black fir trees. I told myself I would never go back to the House, that I'd hide under a rock and hibernate and wait for spring, far away from the Collège, but then a little voice shouted from the front door that the tarte of winter squash was ready, and I must come back. I headed slowly toward the House and on into the entrance hall, unhurriedly removing my muddy shoes. I entered the dining room, where everyone was seated, watching me come in with a faint smile, almost of surprise, as if they'd forgotten I was there, as if I'd been away, deep in the woods, for a very long time. And Harriett's joyful cries mingled with the fumet of the tarte, and the salty steam of soup.

Sunday evenings were gut-wrenching. It's not an image. I suffered physically. The first weekend, since no one knew what was wrong with me, there was talk of calling my teachers first thing in the morning to let them know I was recuperating. As soon as I heard that, I immediately felt better. They then realized my ailment was like the pain of being stateless, like having a phantom limb that still feels numb to the amputee. I returned to the Collège.

One Friday evening when I was particularly happy to be going home, I sat smiling in Petit Père's car on the winding road as it entered our woods, and I caught sight of his mischievous expression in the rearview mirror. He had the amused look of someone who's waiting in the uncomfortable darkness of a theater seat for a show to begin. He wouldn't tell me what was going on.

As soon as we went through the door of the House a strange smell tickled my nostrils. It was the heady essence of a stylish old lady. I knew at once: Great-Aunt Babel had come. I found them all in the salon, Petite Mère, Harriett and Babel, having a lively conversation. Babel was the most romantic woman I've ever known, with a dramatic profile, thick dyed hair, skin veined with white cream, and two emphatic rosy apples on her powdered cheeks. Babel had a smoker's voice, just made to be heard in all the intellectual salons in the City, and everything about her was meant to be noticed, from the lipstick seeping into the corners of her mouth, to her emerald eyes ringed with black. Half dragon, half witch, her nose was even more hooked than those of all the Aberfletches put together, and she was at least as terrifying as she was fascinating. Once we were in the lair of our bedroom, Harriett explained conspiratorially that Babel intended to stay all autumn at the House, as she had sold her apartment in the City because she really didn't spend much time there anymore, between stays at the spa. She had simply knocked on the door that morning with the knob of her heavy cane; a taxi filled with her snakeskin trunks was waiting behind her. They'd hastily granted her the room at the end of the corridor. "She's going to sleep on our floor?" I cried, outraged that we'd been divested of our privilege. Harriett nodded in silence, sheepishly.

The first night was awful; Babel snored like an ogre.

We didn't hear her use the bathroom and yet, in the morning, she came down to the breakfast table looking superb, very smart. We were prepared to believe there was a magic spell at work, and Harriett and I began spying on her closely. We shadowed her during her walks in the garden, where she went, wordlessly, dressed in a long purple cape that caught on the coppery leaves scattered throughout the grass. She went deeper into the cover of trees, without straying, as if she knew where she was going. In her wake danced ginger fairies with golden feet; mushrooms, huddled among the damp roots, glowed dimly on her approach, and the streaming branches opened above her head. It was as if Babel could enchant the forest with her solemn step, and the trees acknowledged her.

Babel spent three consecutive autumns at the House. They were the loveliest autumns of our life. On unpacking her trunks every September, she took away with her all the essence of leaves that are decaying, yet grandiose. She was the spell of the undergrowth, exhaling strong odors of humus peppered with thick moss. She was the shadowy creature who gazed at herself in the black ink of the lake.

At dinner Babel was the only one who spoke, but anyway, what could we have possibly had to say that might have been more interesting, or better articulated? She had the perfect, old-fashioned eloquence of an erudite sophisticate whose knowledge serves only to vie in brilliance with her peers. She had lived an extraordinary life, which fascinated Klaus, Louisa, and even Harriett, but which rather alarmed me. Babel had met the crown princes of extinct dynasties; Babel had traveled on camelback across the dunes of ancient deserts; Babel had been divorced three times and had dozens of lovers. When she is tired of her apartment, Babel takes a suite at the Grand Condé, Place du Palais. She rings the bell at least three times an hour, gives orders, and gets what she wants, and men nevertheless fall in love with her, because she is strong enough to break them. Babel has friends who are witches, yes indeed, they do exist, I assure you, she asserts in her breezy manner, and she tells of potions for relieving menstrual pain that are made from an infusion of ermine's foot. She has seen all the great orchestras, and has advised Klaus, if he must be a trumpet player, to be the best, and even to become a conductor, if he can. She talks about the Opéra Royal, its huge chandeliers, its loges with their heavy curtains. She prefers the symphonies of Smigernsson to the more simplistic rhapsodies of Zibelli-Mostronov, because she sees herself most definitely as belonging to the postdestructuralists. Babel takes another helping of gratin, then continues; she does eat, but never talks with her mouth full, which means she talks continuously. By the time we leave the table, we are both intoxicated and sated, and we can still hear her, grumbling in her sleep, all night long.

In December Babel left for the mountains of the south where she suffocated in the burning vapors of the latest fashionable spa, re-tiled every year according to the current taste. We learned of her passing, without warning, in the dead of winter, from the resort's medical services. I was left, at the age of fifteen, feeling infinitely saddened by her death. We had often sensed we hardly knew Great-Aunt Babel and then, after three hours in her company, we could say we knew her entire life story.

But Great-Aunt Babel is not my little sister.

I cannot speak about her death. But the time has come, the transition is perfect. I have come up against the deep, buried, unspeakable sorrow of a sister losing a sister.

The news of the accident was like the door on an airplane opening mid-flight, an enormous suction of air, unstoppable, toward an infinite void.

It is autumn that killed Harriett, at the dawn of her thirtieth year. It is the leaves sodden with dirty rain, the slippery road winding between two slopes of soggy grass, the bare trees, mineral monoliths of dead life. She was driving fast, they said, as if to exonerate the autumn. But Harriett is not to blame, nor is her car, which she loved, nor her driving, alert and enthusiastic, just as she was, quick and nervous. Harriett, the stream of laughter, her little hand slipping into mine, childish fears trembling behind the terrifying courage of her big dark eyes. Aviatrix and Apache, herbalist and warrior, she is all the strongest women on earth, never a nymph and never a dove, always the bright blade of a cruel smile.

After the news I could do nothing, could say nothing. I stared with horror at the familiar walls, as if they'd been gutted by a cannonball. The autumn wind infiltrated the entire House, I was constantly freezing. My bed, the horrible bed without its twin, so similar to its neighbor, now empty; I loathed it all.

I don't remember much. I went with everyone just as far as the fence surrounding the cemetery, but I couldn't go in, I was held back under the bare trees, by some invisible force, monstrously mute. Paralyzed, I watched from a distance as the hearse spit out its coffin. The wind was screaming words in my ears, and so I curled up in a ball, my head about to explode, and woke up two months later with a mug of coffee before me, a spoon in my hand, and everyone there at the table. I had understood that Harriett no longer existed, and the snow in the orchard covered everything with a heavy layer of salutary amnesia.

I have never forgiven the autumn. Every September my organs begin to function completely on their own, because my mind is loath to bring up to date my experience of a world without Harriett. In autumn my senses hibernate. They wake up in winter, the way they woke up after her death, all of a sudden, the way your hearing is dazzled when you emerge from a tunnel.

From time to time I would open her toy chest and slowly go through everything, all those things that had led to the formation of her brain. Her little infatuations and great passions—the jars of insects where a few dried blades of grass remained, the wooden figurines, the braided ribbons with their faded colors, the talismans made of chestnuts, the notebooks where her sketches of rare scarabs had been painstakingly spread across the pages. Under her bed, stuck in the skirting board, was a sock she'd lost as a child. I left it there. We vacuum around it, but her little foot without its mate stays under the empty mattress. It is there still, that sock, on the first floor of the House, exposed to the raging wind, ensnared by Virginia creeper, the façade slumping with dry rot, no doubt. If I returned there now, and went through the front door, climbed laboriously up the spiral staircase, taking care to avoid the two rotted steps, and carried on along the corridor with the broken stained-glass window, strewn with dead leaves in the worn light of the crazed walls, and went into our little room, I'd find our two beds pushed up against the wall, and Harriett's little sock still stuck in the skirting board. I would sit on her bed, and she would sit by my side, as light as the dawn, and I would feel only her invisible smile dancing against my shoulder. I'd listen to the wind of the summer trees whistling through the broken window pane and tumbling down the corridor, rustling leaves into corners. Harriett would tell me that it was time to go out and play, and she'd fall in step with me and lead me to the woods, me with my cane, she on her perch in the treetops, laughing to see me grown so old.

We should have grown old together, in the House, Harriett and I, each of us in our bed, lying like marble in the light-filled tomb of our bedroom.

I promise, I would have held your little hand in mine.

Winter

It must have been winter. Do you remember, Harriett, the snow was never that immaculate Russian fairytale white? The vegetation in the garden was still luxuriant, beneath the snow, which gave it a hue of icy emerald, while the sun shining on the thick layer of snow scattered it with sequins of gold. In addition, the snow got dirty in no time, plowed by our numb little feet and the swishing runners of our wooden sleds. We opened the window one morning in late November, and the breath of day was taken away, suspended above the trees in a vast sky dappled with wisps of marble. With my hand still gripping the shutter, I shot Harriett a look full of wonder; drawn by the cold light falling from the window, she had already pressed her head against my shoulder to see better. Then we heard Klaus hurrying down the stairs; from high up in his roost he must have seen the snow before we did, and we fussed, because now he'd get there first to sink his boots in its depths. We rushed to the bedroom door, ran down the corridor, pushing and shoving to try and slow each other down, and Louisa opened her door upstairs, shouting to us to wait, but we could hear Klaus's loud laugh already echoing through the entrance hall. As if we were being lashed by his laughter, we belted down the stairs, leapt from step to step, then to a mad confusion of scarves and coats; we could never find our own, so we wore somebody else's, Petite Mère's, Petit Père's, thin, nervous children's calves swimming in too-big boots.

It became an incredible show of battle stations: the boundless world of winter games was open to us at last, and our cozy blanket-warmed sleep was swept away all at once. The autumn torpor suddenly shook itself and yielded to the dizzying excitement of long sled rides, snowball fights, and winter tales by the fire sitting between Petit Père and Petite Mère. I'll never forget the sacred silence of the woods, with their heavy branches, the cavern-like calm which crystallized our breath when we went in under the trees, into the marmoreal arms of the frost-stitched firs. I felt like the mysterious heiress to a once-grandiose empire, wandering slowly under the arches of an immaculate cathedral. I held my breath, and my solitary steps crunched on the heavy mineral fur that covered the world.

We would catch snowflakes in our hands and examine them closely while they melted, inexorably, on our palms, too warm and red . . . The faint numbness which signaled it was time to go home, that weariness in our limbs, inviting us to a sweet sleep in a blanket of ice . . . eyes filling with tears because Klaus threw chunks of hard snow that slid past scarves and down necks . . . snow biting skin with little teeth of ice . . . We knocked the soles of our boots against the porch to loosen fat slabs of coagulated snow, which had taken strange shapes from the tread of the soles.

Like little furry animals huddling together to keep warm, we siblings became physically closer in winter. I would lean over onto Klaus's shoulder, which smelled so sweetly of spice and pine resin, with a slightly smoky odor coming from his brown curls. The rest of the year we almost never touched. Or we would grab each other clumsily by the wrists to dance a sort of waltz in the entrance hall as it sparkled with sunlight, or we'd push and shove along the corridor to hold each other back, or kick someone behind the knees to knock them over. That was our way of showing affection, attachment, the fierce nudges of children who have not yet mastered their bodies. We only touched each other when in motion. But in winter we had the right to stay motionless, our four bodies, individual sources of heat, suddenly came together. Klaus would be on the sofa in the salon, studying the scores he had to prepare for the following week, and his hands, warm and full, with their rather prominent veins, were already those of a man. He didn't mind me looking over his shoulder, with my knees drawn up as far as his armpits, like an organic arm-rest that I was trying to keep as immobile as possible, not to disturb him, not to make him chase me away into another room. Harriett had placed her heavy little head of a genius against my side, and her feet dangled in the void, wiggling whenever something the least bit exciting was happening in the comic book she was devouring. Louisa leaned on Klaus's other shoulder with an already feminine grace, and from a distance they were so lovely, you might have taken them for a modest young couple. I remember how, with our hips joined, shoulders touching, and arms intertwined, I was given the happy impression that we were some sort of deformed four-headed monster, a wonderful chimera that was endlessly recomposing itself, to the crackling of the fire in the hearth.

We all wore sweaters that our great-grandmother had knitted for Petit Père, Hilde, and Bertie. Because she was the darling, with golden hair like Petite Mère's, Louisa wore Petit Père's. It was a royal blue knit with a yellow and white stripe that ran along the shoulders. Klaus had Bertie's, which was logical, because the flamboyant pine green together with a purple and orange edging suited both their characters, not to mention their complexions. I had Hilde's, which didn't particularly enthrall me, with its fine azure stitches crowded between white and turquoise threads. Petite Mère must have fashioned an additional sweater for Harriett, who didn't have one, and the stitches, which were very irregular, added to her casual, clown-like appearance, yellow chick with red pom-poms. These sweaters were taken from the trunk at the beginning of October, and stayed with us every winter. They seemed to grow with us, as if the mysterious great-grandmother, whom we'd never known, had knit them with magical stitches that stretched over our shoulders like a second skin as we grew. There was a sinister side to this, in knowing that the hands that had made these garments were now being digested by the juices of death under eighteen shovelfuls of earth. To think that Hilde had once worn my sweater, that she was a little girl like me, and then she changed and grew up was a slightly terrifying thought. I was afraid I might, through some sort of evil spell cast on anyone who wore this sweater, turn into the same cold-eyed woman raising an arrogant son on her own in the City after a catastrophic divorce.

My eyes are cold now, no doubt. They're no longer the color of a dirty pond, are they, veiled by cataracts and melancholy, a frozen lake under a mauve sky. They're filled with the past and have used up all their sparks. I no longer even try to re-light them. How can I light them, anyway, amid this ballet of lab coats and helpful ghosts who put food on my plate, turn on my television, and speak very loudly in my ear? Here there are no more flower beds or dazzling skies, there's no sparkling snow. The coffee in the cup is cold, like my heart. Time to drink it, get it over with.

Petit Père is the king of hot chocolate. He makes it better than anyone. People in the City would pay an exorbitant amount for a taste of it. As for the king himself, he asks if we'd like something hot to drink, with a tiny wave of mischief curling his thin lips. It's the sign that he's going to make his famous hot chocolate. Not only is it delicious, it's also lovely to behold, hot streams of brown foam swirling in the spoon we hold with the tips of our fingers, eyes glued to the fragrant eddies that makes our nostrils quiver. As Petite Mère, Louisa, and Harriett babble distractedly, a faint smile comes to my lips above my cup, and

I feel good, with my elbows on the rough kitchen table, and the faint rattling of the family dishes—the melodious, banal inflections of the people I've been with since birth, these people who make up my world and my being: the House's little tribe. When I close my eyes, snatches of conversations come back to me—more bursts of voices than constructed sentences, certain words and particular expressions, inarticulate intonations, which seem to echo from deep in the woods. But there is one voice that I cannot quite grasp, and it is the most important of all—I cannot put my finger on Harriett's words. It's as if my memory had evacuated everything that enabled me to hold a lasting impression of them. It's as if a gauze of forgetfulness had preserved me from the suffering caused by her death. But I'm angry with my brain for assuming it has the right to sort through my memories for me. I don't want to remember Great-Aunt Babel's nasal grumbling. I want to hear my little sister humming as she hangs Christmas decorations all over the cold entrance hall. I want to visualize her gestures, skillful or clumsy, ingenious or ingenuous, which every winter transformed our three floors into a golden nest. Harriett was the fairy behind the red snowflakes hanging in the windows, the glittering garlands draping the corridors. If summer was my time to shine, when my being dissolved into the warm air to embrace it fully, Christmas was Harriett's. She radiated and twirled like a devilish elf, her pockets full of cinnamon cookies. Every year she created new rituals; it was, moreover, thanks to her that we placed the figurines on the mantelpiece. She must have been five or six years old when, rummaging in the toy chests in the attic, she came upon a colored metal box filled with painted wooden figurines, men and women and children in faded colors. She took them out, fascinated in a way only a child can be with strange objects. She chose six that represented us, in her opinion. Petit Père was a policeman, standing tall and proud; Little Mother a florist, with spots of bright color and a bun at the base of her neck. Klaus's figurine was a medieval king, who seemed to be a good king, as majestic as a lion. I don't remember Louisa's very well; I think it was something like a pretty shepherdess. Harriett had chosen our figurines with the greatest of care. She'd observed all the remaining characters, holding them very close to her face, turning them this way and that in her febrile little fingers. Suddenly she had a triumphant look in her eyes. I would be the Native American princess with her braids shining in the varnished wood, and she would be an explorer—she took her figurine to Petite Mère and asked her to paint over some of it, transforming the male adventurer into a female one. Petite Mère had to scrape off the varnish to add little touches of flesh-colored paint to hide the explorer's mustache. She added a little red to the lips, and Harriett skipped around the House holding her figurine to her heart. She later decreed that these figurines were our sacred statuettes, to be placed above the fireplace every winter, like a crèche, and that we six were the entire universe. We very willingly complied with her adorable whim. Every winter thereafter, once the first snows had fallen, Harriett ran up to the attic to fetch our figurines. She cherished them, made herself dizzy uttering shamanic chants and fantastical prayers as she stood by the hearth. Bright flames of light from the fire wrapped the statuettes in a golden halo that slid over their faces frozen in eternal smiles. With each murmured psalm, Harriett's gaze plunged into the fireplace in the hearth, and she sought so earnestly to instill the figurines with powers that I do believe, in the end, she managed to breathe life into them, along with our souls. Because when Harriett died and we stopped putting the figurines on the mantelpiece, as if by coincidence a terrible chill smothered my guts.

The dazzling images blind me, and the snow-frosted grassy slopes plunge beneath the fir trees. It is the light of a bare bulb, the steel of a blade, not the virginal white of summer dresses, nor the white paint dulled by daylight on the façade of the House. It's a livid white of silence, and all life is contrasted against it—the black, blue crows; footsteps that dirty; pink calves in huge boots. A whiteness that pierces eardrums, burns retinas. And our sleds racing under the branches, our hearts pounding, because we're heading too fast in among the trees, and there's a stream flowing at the bottom of the slope, and the stream is deep. And so we decide we've had enough, we hold our feet out, brake as hard as we can, our boots plowing into the snow to slow us down, and the spume of snow that flies up when we fall cuts our cheeks with a thousand tiny bites. Klaus always went too far, we could see him from the top of the hill, and he disappeared into the trees, all alone and tiny, a faint black rabbit against the bluish snow of the undergrowth. His triumphant cry of a boy king made the treetops shiver with a sudden flight of crows. Louisa and I fell early on, terrified by the stream beyond the trees, and I rolled over onto my side with the sled. My head was spinning, my fingers cold and numb, the silence and sudden solitude of the sled that had come to a stop under the trees. A glance behind me, from far away my sisters and Klaus are waving to tell me to come back up, it was their turn, Hurry up Isadora, you're so slow. All at once it's very cold. And the slope has become a hill, and seems steeper than ever before, a white wall standing below the House, a solid wave traversed by quick shadows of cloud.

Harriett was the most agile. She'd taken off on the sled before we even had time to see her get on it. In the blink of an eye she was already speeding through the trees. Of course we should have told her to go more slowly, we should have kept an eye on her, but instead we were always amazed by her vivacity, and she was like a playful imp, and we encouraged her to go even faster, to slalom between the trees, to overtake us all, to stop only when she'd gone as far as possible. That afternoon, when suddenly we didn't see her at the end of the field, our faces, pale with incomprehension and fear, turned toward the forest, waiting for her tiny form to emerge, laughing. Then at the same time we all understood, and ran as fast as we could. I was terrified and exhausted, and the snow was up to our knees, stopping us from going faster, like a rough sea pulling us into the swell. Klaus was the first to reach the stream. When I got there, Harriett was shivering, weeping in his arms, her drenched hair clinging to her temples in thick clumps of bluish lovelocks.

Everyone laughed about the incident. The others called it "Harriett's great drenching." And every year they told the story, as soon as the first snows came. Harriett laughed, and said it would never happen again, she was much better now at controlling the sled, she could go even faster and stop just before she reached the stream. But I said nothing, my fists clenched with anguish under the table, and I recalled the boundless abyss that had opened in my guts when I suddenly could not see her on her sled at the bottom of the slope. The sensation of my breath suddenly being sucked out of me. That teetering on the edge of the void, the voice being torn from me, my eyes staring wildly at a white field of nothingness. I saw myself, alone, at that moment, while the others were already scrambling down the embankment to go to her rescue. That day I caught a glimpse of what my life would be like without my little sister.

When I heard about the pouring rain, and the dead leaves sliding across the road, and the car rammed into the side of the mountain, I immediately thought she'd had a sledding accident. It was idiotic, but in my mind—so staggered by the news—we were children in winter, and she always rode too quickly across the snowy plain. And I felt myself tipping once again into the void. I feel it still, today.

Winters without Harriett—either because she was wandering the globe, or was already dead—increasingly resembled long marches toward death. Snowflakes no longer seemed to whirl joyfully the way they used to, when my little sister and I stayed with our noses against the pane, dazzled by their fluffy dance. Now they drifted slowly through a gray sky, and landed flat and heavy on the already-whitened grass.

It had also been in winter that I turned down Oktav's proposal of marriage. The Pont-Noir bridge was all white under the white sky and the white City, and little crystals clung to the shoulders of his big navy blue sailor's jacket. He spread his arms for me to nestle against him, I knew by heart the smell bundled in his scarf. It would have been so easy to burrow into his comforting mint-scented breath, and to say yes, I want to marry you. To kiss his mouth as if it were candy, to feel his lips on mine expanding into a smile, that kind of irrepressible smile that makes a deep kiss impossible but is delicious all the same.

I sometimes wonder what became of Oktav. Not that I regret turning him down, but I'm curious to know what his life was like, after me. I'm sure he must have found a new love. He was quick to love, and readily grew attached, because he was a charming man. He was funny, and lively, so of course he must have easily taken to another woman's skin, run his fingers through another woman's hair. There was a time when the very thought enraged me, but now that I'm old and rather ugly, I tell myself I would have grown weary of him, sooner or later. He would have put on weight, become a grouch. He would have wanted children, no doubt, and I never saw myself as a mother, only a daughter and a sister. I was a reasonably good daughter, not very affectionate, but I think I was an exceptional sister. I wish I were still a sister.

Everything began to gather pace when Petit Père died, shortly before I turned forty and a few years after Harriett's accident. I was very glad I didn't have a husband breathing down my neck, who would have stopped me from taking over the House. He would have burdened me with sensible advice, no doubt, would have preferred to leave this old House behind: it only wears people out and eats up savings. Instead, on my own, I was able to stand up to the entire family. We gathered one weekend in December. Petit Père's will, unsurprisingly, revealed that he was leaving the House to me. It was logical, almost a foregone conclusion, without any apparent drama; I'd been living there alone with him for a few years already, whereas everyone else had migrated to bigger cities, or garish seaside dwellings. We sat down, Louisa, Klaus, Uncle Bertie, Suzy, Aunt Hilde and the cousins, around that big festive dining room table, now full for the first time in a very long while. The sorrow of seeing that we were so much less joyful than before, and how pale our faces were in this light that had once been so warm . . . We were so silent, so awkward around that table that we could hear the creaking in the walls and in the roof. No one dared speak, no one dared evoke the future of this big old shack. Everyone there, with the exception of Suzy, had learned to walk on these floorboards. Uncle Bertie's eyes were moist and his face was gaunt with mourning. My eyes filled with tears to see him grieving for his little brother in this way, so similar to my own mourning for my little sister. I recognized his grief; we were like two soldiers from the same regiment, smiling faintly at each other as we lay dying in a rotting trench. We eventually began to speak, our words weighty and hoarse. In the beginning they hardly dared contradict me when I asserted that it was out of the question to sell our House. Then Hilde was the first to bring up the overall condition of the building and the cost of any eventual repairs. Aleksander, who'd become even drier than his mother, came out with a few figures, printed neatly and legibly on a white sheet of paper blackened on the upper left-hand side by the seal of his notarial office, as if by a thick opaline fly. I hardly listened. Nearly all of them spoke, except

Louisa who, with her head tilted to one side, her cheeks hollow, was considering me from under her eyelashes. We gazed at each other in silence while everyone around the table was beginning to get restless. Quite suddenly, teeth clenched but with surprising vehemence, Louisa burst out: "She won't sell." She got to her feet and said again that I wouldn't sell and that this meeting was a waste of time. That she could read my gaze and that I'd already made up my mind. She was right. They acted a bit annoyed for a while then, on the doorstep, wished me good luck in keeping it afloat, this dump that was over a hundred years old. Only Klaus had anything vaguely kind to say. I stood on the porch, once they'd all driven away. The breeze was stirring the dead leaves that had blown against the stone steps. A great silence arose from the forest, off to my right, and the dry resin of the kingly fir trees tasted fleetingly of steel. I pulled my shawl tighter around my chest and went back into the House. The front door closed heavily behind me, and its dull thud rose to the floors above and reverberated like a growl throughout the hall. It was done. I was alone in the House.

Winter went by very quickly, with all the inheritance issues to be settled, the inventory of repairs to be done in the spring: changing the boiler, reinforcing the roof, and installing thicker windowpanes in the green bathroom on the first floor. The wind blew in there, and the tiles, a dormant basin of luminous water, were freezing. I began by selling the farm we owned near the village, which no longer brought in very much, because we'd donated most of our shares to the market farmers who worked there. I got enough from it to pay for the repairs. The other two plots of land that belonged to us, woods on the other side of the canton, were fairly lucrative during hunting season, thanks to the game tax we'd introduced. We had the stags to thank for running over our moss every year. As regards the rest of our income, which had meant a good part of the family didn't have to work, in exchange for a few sacrifices, it consisted of a small apartment in the City, which we rented for an exorbitant amount to desperate students, as well as a few shares in a seaside hotel chain. In addition to all that, I simply let the fortune I'd inherited from Great-Aunt Babel bear fruit, as it had been carefully invested, and I pawned a few of her fur coats. At the end of the day, when darkness filled the windows, I sat back in my chair. My gaze slipped over Petit Père's desk, where a photograph of us as children—in which I looked absolutely horrible—was gathering dust. The evenings were all alike; I dragged myself into the kitchen, checked the pantry to see what was left in the way of canned meals, and heated up either a stew or a soup in my favorite saucepan, the high-sided white one, with its trim of old-fashioned flowers. How many soups had we boiled in there? I went up to bed after sipping my herbal tea in silence, in the salon by the fire. My little bed was made up next to Harriett's cold one. I was not so foolish as to murmur good night to her; I knew very well she was dead, but in the end I did smooth her untouched sheets with the flat of my hand. Slight creases turned up there from time to time, as if someone had been sitting there. I switched off the light and complete darkness fell all through the House. A tomb-like silence, opaque and terrible, filled it from cellar to attic.

I spent one more winter alone in the House, and this time the solitude hit me full-on. When I came back from the woodpile and looked up at the House looming over me, all white in the middle of the garden of snow, I thought I saw a light come on in a window on the first floor and, framed behind the curtain, a familiar face. There was no one, and now my boots were all alone in a row to themselves when I set them down by the doormat.

At the beginning of the following autumn, I placed a classified ad in the regional newspaper, "Seeking tenant for the winter, big heated house, quiet, garden, privacy respected." The baker assured me she'd post my offer at the train station in the City, the next time she went to see her son.

Rusbrock, my tenant, arrived on 20 November. A herbalist, like Harriett, how odd. That's what I told him, when he introduced himself, before we toured the House. Well then, your sister and I can talk about local plants. I don't think so, Monsieur, I don't think so. He didn't question me further. He had lived, like me. He must've been not quite ten years older than I was, a charming ten years that situated him just in the right place, to fill in for my absent older brother and dead father. Rusbrock was pragmatic, decently intelligent. He appreciated the fact I was well into my thirties, I liked his deep, warm voice, which had something liquid and briny about it, as if he'd swallowed a river. His long nose made him likable, and his slightly rounded back would have drained all the charisma from him were it not for the reddish skin of his large paws, the hands of a gardener, caressing. I hadn't been with a man since Oktav—nearly fifteen years? The touch of a warm palm sliding over my skin was enough to arouse the sleeping grain of my epidermis, to make the blonde down of my naked flanks against the sheets stand on end. My hips were a bit rounder than the last time an arm had held them, because I was closer to forty than to thirty. We only made love in his room, Suzy and Bertie's old room. Out of the question to defile my childhood bedroom, to trouble the peaceful games Harriett and I once played.

Rusbrock, through who knows what sort of sylvan magic that causes forest people to recognize one another, blended wonderfully into the woods of my childhood. He did not clash, as Oktav had done, with my familiar landscape. His eyes were the color of damp moss, his cheekbones were pinkish like burgeoning buds (broken veins), his shoulders were broad, and strong, fit to carry the logs for the fireplace. My cup of tea at my lips, through the little distorting windowpanes in the kitchen I watched as he walked off into the garden. His strange build seemed to undulate, all brown against the morning snow. A few minutes later I heard the door of the shed groan on its hinges, and Rusbrock's panting, rasping breath as he re-cut the tree stumps. I watched as he held the axe, with the confident gestures of a man who splits wood as naturally as he breathes. He came back in, his lips sticky with foam, which he wiped off roughly in his elbow before placing a little kiss on my forehead. His hand would crush the hair at the base of my neck, and he always spilled a little tea when he filled his cup. The lilac snow outside was reflected in the drops of amber liquid on the wood.

The winter went by like a familiar dream, dreamt every night. We woke, in the morning, each of us in our own bed, since I went back to my childhood room after our nocturnal languor. I could never stand sleeping with someone in my bed, and moreover, Rusbrock breathed too heavily. Great-Aunt Babel beat him on that score, however, back in the day.

During the night I would forget I was not alone in the House. That must be what made it possible for Rusbrock and me to put up with each other all winter long. Every morning my eyelids opened onto a flow of white light from the garden. I got up, pushed back the shutters—snow or no snow, still cold; I coughed a little as I put on my bathrobe. The parquet creaked under my slippers, and it was when I came out into the corridor and saw the open doors, and could hear the rasping sound of a razor blade on a man's skin coming from the green bathroom that I remembered Rusbrock. I was happy then, inexplicably happy, to be made aware of that life at the end of the corridor. Slowly I opened the door to the bathroom and Rusbrock, red and pink against the glossy emerald tiles, was leaning toward the mirror. He smiled on seeing me behind him in the reflection. He smelled nice, of eau de Cologne, and his skin still shone from the bath he'd just had. The tiles were already losing their layer of vapor, because he liked his bath only barely lukewarm. With one hand he took his razor away from his face, with the other he pulled me toward him to place a kiss on my forehead. I narrowed my eyes in a smile. The milky water in the sink eddied when he unplugged the drain, and he slapped his big palms full of balm on his raw cheeks. He pinched my ribs, followed me along the corridor, and we went down to breakfast.

I loved to watch him devouring his charred bread, I could tell he was in rude good health, thanks to me, for he had all the insouciance of the man who is satisfied in his body, the man who has enjoyed the night's lovemaking and who asks himself no questions. And then, all of a sudden, that smugness was unbelievably annoying. One morning I looked at him devouring his tartine, and I realized that winter was coming to an end and that not once, as I ate my tartine, had this man looked at me with joy. I realized he didn't really care, and that our lovemaking would be the same every night, a sort of ransom for his good services during the day, the moment that would make up for an afternoon spent chopping wood. February made me understand how much I did not love Rusbrock, how much I did not like making love with Rusbrock, or drinking tea with Rusbrock, or talking with Rusbrock.

Gradually his callous palms became unbearable to me. He caressed as if he were smoothing the folds of a tablecloth, in jerky little motions with the flat of the hand. I began to feel how horrible it was, for my skin's sake. In the morning, in the little green bathroom with the window that jammed, I found myself alone in the viscous bathtub, and I shivered with disgust as I rubbed the soap over my belly. That was where he had put his ugly hands, his ugly lips. He repulsed me when he wandered around the House, with his heavy step; the House creaked with his weight. He made himself at home everywhere—in the salon, in the garden, in me. One day when he came back from the woods, after a solitary walk in the snow, he told me how much he liked being in this place. It was this factor that revealed and made me understand everything that was wrong, everything that bothered me. He loved the House; he and I had become rivals. He dared to point out to me, to *me*, as if he were the first to have observed with such love how skillfully that gable on the southwest side had been wrought, or how exceptional this or that tree in the orchard was. He tried to make himself as legitimate here as I was—I who had grown up here, who had the House in my blood, who had spent my whole life inside these walls. One fine day I replied frostily that he'd do better not to love the House, because he would be leaving before spring. Never would the House, nor I, belong to him. Rusbrock would not become a landlord; he would stay a tenant, forever merely passing through. His broad back went out the door for the last time in mid-February. He forgot a pair of briefs on the edge of the bathtub, for the sake of one last display of crudeness.

One should always beware of winter loves. It's the body's survival instinct calling out for another warm body to snuggle up against. As soon as the snow melts, everything reappears in its naked truth, in its earliest greenery of young grass.

That was the first and last winter tenant I ever had.

The winters that followed were, in a way, the ones I had always expected. The unprecedented experience of radical solitude, the challenge I set myself every year now, with a shiver of pleasure, when the first flurries fell, intensifying my reclusion. The road, muffled beneath hardening snow night after night by intense spells of cold, formed the impenetrable wall of my castle. I could have asked the municipality to come up the hill to salt the road, and thus make it accessible, which would have allowed me to go to the village for shopping. But I didn't. I secretly looked forward to transforming the House into a palace of ice, which gave me the impression of being absolutely alone in the world, in this white, empty countryside where, from time to time, a single crow might caw. The deep silence of the snowy woods, the uniform fields unfurled at the foot of the hill, completely erased the existence of others. During those terrible winters, I truly was the only mistress of the world around me. Winter worked a spell, and left us alone, the House and me.

I was a shadow, in winter. The shadow of a ghoul, a harpy, a banshee, whatever, a creature that doesn't even know if it is alive. Meals on my own, the great silence of the empty House, the banging of radiators, the gurgling in my stomach, everything became both noisier and more silent. The noises the House made seemed organic, and my own breathing sounded mechanical, calculated, artificial. I had no one to listen to, and so I would stop myself sometimes, seized with an inane doubt, to take my pulse and listen carefully to my breathing. I was suddenly afraid that, without realizing, I'd become a ghost, that I had slid soundlessly into non-existence. I was startled by my reflection in the mirror, found myself horrible, ugly, and old. I told myself that if I'd seen myself like that as a little girl, I would have thought I was seeing a witch, and I laughed with amazement as I felt my tight skin. I was captivated by my sunken cheeks, cold hands, bluish lips. So this was who she was as an adult, that Isadora Aberfletch, the adult I sometimes thought about as a child lying in bed. I'd never been afraid of growing old, but I was curious. What would I look like, would my hair be dirty gray or luminous white? To see myself grown old, now, has always been strange. I look at myself and can no longer find the image of who I was as a little girl. I can of course resort to some mental process to erase my wrinkles, fill my cheeks, enliven my eyes, all to try and call up my former features. But it's always a mystification, there's nothing but a rose-colored blur, an ingenuous lie. The truth is we can't remember our face. We reconstitute it imperfectly, just like, as children, we used to entertain ourselves in the mirror, wrinkling our skin, imagining what we'd look like when we got old. But all this me, me, me—it makes me sick of myself, I'm becoming bloated. Ever since I've been living alone in the House, and the notion of "we" has vanished, and even more so now that I'm in this institution, the "I" is omnipresent and I can't stand it anymore. I was so much happier when I had something else to observe besides my own self.

Winter made me hyper-aware of my being, that otherness of the body, that strangeness. The snow dazzled like the dizziness of thoughts that are too profound, of ideas that hold no pleasure. I wallowed in a state of such intense solitude that I forgot the House was inhabited, even by myself. I laughed to see myself teetering on the edge of reason, aware only of the glaring whiteness all around that pierced my temples; the opaque silence that deafened my eardrums.

I do think, however, that I liked being alone. I could explore other selves. There were days when I was queen. The House belonged to me in its entirety, a good fire going in the hearth, and the conducts that intertwined on each floor transported a fierce, strong, sharp heat, with a taste of pine. The walls vibrated with gentle, intimate warmth, I turned on all the little lamps, and then there were great streams of yellow into the subdued light of the rooms. The lampshades filtered a calming orange light into the air, and seemed to pulse, luminous mushrooms standing on pedestal tables. The chandeliers, flakes of champagne, shone like the warm throats of miniature dragons. My palace was brilliant, it was good to live there, so warm, in a universal hideout against the cold of the sky. I was the sole survivor of an endless night. I felt proud, able to live without anyone, without others of my kind, just the brown hardwood floor, the heavy curtains that warmed the windows, and the incandescent lightbulbs. I reigned over all these little furnishings with the majesty of an empress, and I took the last of Great-Aunt Babel's cloaks to drape over my shoulders. The transformation was complete. On my fiftysomething body, on my hips that were already flabby, even though they'd never borne a child, the folds of ermine beat like a drum. I appreciated the weight of the dead creatures on my back. I took slow steps from one end of the House to the other, and the train of fur followed me like a heavy, slithering serpent. Wild animals, camphor wood, burning pine, and steaming bread, I filled the House with warmth and light. I was its vital force, the organ throbbing in a thorax of beams and gables.

There were other days when no fur coat would have sufficed to hearten the empty space inside my ribcage, where the black exhalations of a dull terror lurked. Winter was eating away at my mental health, bit by bit, with each white morning, with each glare of harsh light. The silence was becoming unbearable, I heard it when it didn't exist, all around me. I had auditory hallucinations. I sometimes heard steps crunching on the hard snow, I leapt up from my armchair to press my eye against the pane, febrile, and a cold sweat ran down my spine. I was breathless as my gaze searched the bare horizon and the edge of the black woods. The tall trees were not at all familiar or welcoming anymore. Disgusted by their scrawny, barren branches, I would gladly have had them all chopped down. The garden was ugly. The snow made everything wet, crunching, running in rivulets. Even birdsong became inaudible. They startled me in my hibernal lethargy, with a sudden screeching that cut through the cold air. I was on edge. For entire days, sometimes, I convinced myself, nearly as aware of the irrationality of the thing as I was deeply troubled by the possibility of its reality, that I was surrounded by ghosts. These were the dead souls of my family—the icy hand of my mother gripping my hair at my nape and pressing me against the back of the armchair. "You didn't help me die," she whispered in my ear, which was buzzing with solitude.

But I never felt threatened by Harriett's ghost. I imagined it gliding around me, pacing the corridors and rooms as if to make sure everything was still in its place. The floorboards complaining overhead were almost reassuring. I recognized my invisible little sister's dancing steps as she ran through the attic. Harriett still loved me, from deep within her coffin.

From time to time my thoughts were abruptly interrupted by the sour jangling of the telephone. It was Louisa, asking me if the winter wasn't too rough at the House, if I had anyone coming to visit. I replied that I did; she left me alone. She told me about the skiing trip to the mountains she and her second husband were planning, those same mountains where Great-Aunt Babel used to go to take the waters. There was luxury snow there, and mystical summits; her husband prided himself on going cross-country, from time to time. Her little Kurt was doing well at university; she thought he had a girlfriend, but couldn't really be sure. I mumbled my monosyllabic replies, choked with awkwardness. Louisa's phone calls did, however, secretly make me happy. Our relationship was relatively cool, we each had so much hidden scorn for the other's choices in life. But while we didn't understand one another, we coexisted in spite of everything, and it was a pleasure to realize this. "We'll come to the House when the weather's fine," she said. And that was it. I put the phone down, and felt empty. Behind me, a curtain moved. I turned around abruptly, heart pounding, eyes staring with horror at the thick velvet. There was nothing. There never was anything.

Klaus didn't call often, but he still called more often in winter than the rest of the year. In winter he took up residence in this or that capital, where he was conducting the orchestra for

Christmas concerts. He was vaguely composing, ordered whisky up to his suite, and thought now and again of his little sister, deep in the countryside of his childhood. Klaus's calls always left me very fragile, on the verge of tears, very much alone. He was my beloved older brother, whom I'd always admired, and the genuine warmth in his voice always made me feel immediately at home. Klaus, unlike Louisa, was not afraid of talking about the past, and I loved it when we would reminisce for an hour or two on the telephone about our childhood, our summers. It was as if something began to dazzle in the House when this happened, I felt a happiness close to tears, to be there in our family seat, sole guardian of the temple. This awful happiness made us voluble; we roared with laughter as we recalled our misadventures, or rediscovered some small wonder of our childhood years. We almost managed to talk about Harriett now without sadness. She was a part of our memories in the same way that she'd been a part of our lives: her joy, her sulks, her curiosity lived on, as if superimposed, the moment we said her name—Harriett, with that final click of the consonant against the teeth, was the magic word that embellished our conversations. She was the guarantor of a past that, for all of us, had been the most beautiful time in our lives. When we hung up, the House seemed inhabited once again. I leaned toward the hearth, the way I used to, and Harriett, Louisa, and Klaus came to place their little faces next to mine, to contemplate the fire, fascinated by the dance of the flames. They shoved me with their sharp hips, to try and have the best spot by the fire, where it was warmest. Let's all get warm together while the wood's burning and the fire's crackling.

There is a fireplace in the common room here. When I leave my bedroom, that's where I go, but I think the director of the care home is trying to save money, because they never light the fire. So I go back along the tiled corridors that echo with the breathing of the dying.

My first winter without the House will soon be here. I can hardly imagine it. Snow without fir trees, the cold without the comforting volume of familiar rooms, the winter festivities without Harriett's figurines on the mantelpiece. There will be nothing to look forward to anymore, in the days to come. Nothing sparkles, nothing warms me within. I'm like the House, collapsing among the trees.

I know I can't stretch in my sheets anymore, because my limbs are numb. Unable to stretch—yet what should I do? I'm a memory, a world. Inside me, little Klaus, Louisa, and Harriett are running, with their gaze the color of a murky pond. Those children live only in me now.

I reminisce, all day long, I think and think, I see, without reliving. I repeatedly experience the failure of my memories, the imperfection of memory itself. I forget things, they will surface no more, and the enterprise seems doomed from the start.

I dip constantly into the lukewarm waters of the lake among the willows, Uncle Bertie's hidden lake, and on summer mornings, at the breakfast table Suzy is pink, in her silk peignoir. Bertie's hand rests on her neck, he's playing with her hair. They are tender, and happy, and dead. If I die, when will they live again? For whom will they play, eternally, those mornings of love in the House, if not for me, who summons them again and again?

Here, they bring the trays to my room. I've never seen what the kitchens are like, nor who prepares my meals. I recognize the dishes they serve because I've eaten them elsewhere, prepared by someone else, at some point in the past. Petite Mère made ancestral dishes, meat that simmered and vegetables that boiled, all of that because someone, one day thousands of years ago, decided to chop a slain animal into little pieces and mix it in a pot on the fire with water from where the fish swam and little polished pebbles rolled. Fish have always swum, apparently. They come down rivers without knowing where those rivers lead, they get lost in the meanders, in the green light of the flowing waters.

Here they cook fish in the oven, the flesh is firm and golden with juice. At the House we made fish in cream, and Petite Mère would tell Petit Père to go to the cellar and fetch a handful of special herbs that hung drying in long bouquets of blue branches, which she would then chop finely and toss into the cream. Louisa adored fish, we gladly let her have our portions. Petit Père grumbled a bit, he reminded us that this little fish on our plate had given its life for us, and we would roll our eyes toward the ceiling. Klaus imitated the fish, to make Harriett laugh, then she acted the fish in turn, we hopped away from the table wiggling our arms like fins, like this, and we glided from room to room as if we were swimming.

Klaus had wonderful voices for every character he created. He was very funny, very quick-witted, like a fish quickly darting away into the grasses of the lake.

The night is deep blue, the shutters are closed. Harriett and I are in our beds, in our pajamas, we haven't switched the bedside lamp off yet; I want to read. Klaus suddenly opens the door, leaps into the room and shouts, like an offended princess, "I gave my life for you!" And he rushes toward us, embracing us, and we laugh so hard we cry. He goes back out just as suddenly, and we roll in our sheets pretending to be fish, overexcited when we should be sleeping. We hear him running up the stairs, and Louisa cries out, surprised, laughing, and we can vaguely hear Klaus the fish's funny voice repeating Petit Père's words, and we burst out laughing again, Harriett and I, tucked neatly in our little beds.

I sleep well here. But I don't laugh before switching off the light. The room is yellow and nightfall doesn't help matters, it only makes the yellow look dirtier, fills it with wolves, and nightmares, and migraines. Who chose the wallpaper for this old people's home? The same director who won't allow the fire to be lit in the common room?

But it's not all bad. I know that some of the residents have become friends and meet up to play cards, and are on a first-name basis with their care workers. They're making the mistake of adapting. If I adapt, I'm afraid I'll forget this isn't my home.

I thought I'd adapted to winters on my own in the House. I thought I had enough strength and memories to inhabit all the silent floors. I thought that, drained by the experience of my invasive tenant, I'd become an independent woman. I could feel the decades whitening my hair, tightening my skin. I felt I had an armor of deep convictions, and I was determined to let no one encounter my House ever again.

One year, however, I did decide to interrupt my winter solitude. As I'd understood I couldn't live with anyone, I agreed to share my life with strangers, but this time only mentally. In the autumn of my sixty-third year, I joined a book club by correspondence. Every week the committee sent the same book to several readers, who would write a review for publication in the newspaper, discussing that week's novel. In the beginning, this was a way for me to replenish my library and use my writing skills. I was even quite proud when I saw my name in print in the paper for the first time, next to a faithful re-transcription of my opinion of the poetry collection we'd been reading. After the third or fourth publication I realized that my reviews, and those of one other reader, were always noticeably similar, regardless of the book we were describing. I liked her style, and I could tell that, like me, she was not all that young. The reviews were signed Jésabel S. She seemed so close to me that I called the editorial offices to request the contact information for this mysterious alter ego. As they took this for nothing more than an innocent infatuation on the part of an old lady, they raised no objections, and gave me this Jésabel's address. I checked a guide book. She lived right in the center of the City. I was almost disappointed to learn that my alter ego was a citydweller. I nearly gave up my secret friendship with her, figuring that she would hardly understand my tastes, my love for the woods and for my House. I told myself that our lives were too different. I left the paper with her contact information on the desk, and didn't look at it again until December. It hadn't snowed for two days, and the bright sun had melted the blanket of crystal, transforming it into gold-dusted mud. I drank some verbena tea and felt full of light. I went up to the study, and was not as breathless as usual. Then I wrote a letter addressed to Jésabel Skatander, 4 rue du Vieux-Lierre, in the City. I looked at the cream-colored envelope in my hand, the weight of the paper, the cheerful figure of the stamp, and the fine loop I'd given the letter J of Jésabel; they seemed like that many encouraging signs. I went down to the village, dropped the letter into the flap of the mailbox, and let the employee in charge of the mail know that this year I would agree to have my road salted, to allow the mail carrier to come. He gave a faint smile; I don't know if it was in response to the effort I'd just made to connect the rest of the world to the House, or to my outmoded coat. But the fact remains that the very next day a municipal crew was busy all along the hill and from the window in the study I could see them, tossing handfuls of salt along the gleaming road.

Next came the waiting. Now that nothing could prevent a reply from my mysterious correspondent from reaching me, other potential obstacles tormented me. What if the newspaper had given me the wrong address? What if she'd moved in the meantime? Or if she found my undertaking ridiculous and had nothing but scorn for the countryside? And what if, finally, she didn't like the smell of fir trees or the taste of chervil in an omelet? Then what? I was afraid of being deeply disappointed, of some divergence arising abruptly between us that would sweep aside the incredible like-mindedness that had connected us through the club's literary review.

Finally, at the end of a short week, I saw the mail carrier come up the hill in his car, leave something in the letterbox, and drive away. My heart pounding, I went down the spiral staircase four steps at a time and, as dizzy as a big clumsy stag beetle, I put on my gardening boots, and hobbled down to the metal box. Hidden at the bottom, in a steel splash of white daylight, was a gray-blue parcel. I held it close in the morning chill and returned to the House. A wave of familiar warmth enveloped me when I closed the door and, as if in a dream, my eyes staring at the small, cramped handwriting with my name and address, I took off my boots and my coat and went into the salon, where I collapsed into the armchair. The "I" in Isadora was straight and firm, and a slight flourish had been sketched on the "A" in Aberfletch. I opened the parcel. There were two things, and both brought tears to my eyes: a two-page letter, and a book. The book, believe it or not, was Amber Gardano's *Secret Glory*. My favorite book, my childhood book, that story that turned out to be so significant, about the little princess fleeing her father's counselors through the palace because she did not want to be married. I hurried to read the letter, I needed an explanation. I had not mentioned this book to her. My letter, to be honest, had been fairly timid, I'd just briefly told her about the House, and how I found our reviews in the newspaper quite similar, and this made me curious. Her letter was generous, bountiful. By the time I reached the end of her missive, Jésabel had become the best friend I could have hoped for, besides Harriett of course.

She was roughly ten years older than me, which meant older than seventy. Our similarities turned out to extend beyond a simple concordance of taste in literature. She was unmarried, always had been, yet she'd had a child, stillborn. She'd lived her entire life in the same apartment where she'd grown up.

Her view gave onto the trees of a very old cemetery that spread across a gentle slope of bright green lawn dotted with black butterflies. The trees were hardy from the soil of the dead. Her apartment was exceptional, she said, and had barely changed since her childhood, because she liked old things and faded tapestries. She had precise rituals, favorite spots, particularly the window ledge piled with cushions where she liked to sit and read. She was a very bad cook. Most of the time, she ordered her meals from the delicatessen on the corner. She loved her street the way I loved my woods. It was narrow and winding, blackish and medieval, and the shop signs in wrought iron made a sinister rattle in the wind. The streetlamps were over one hundred years old, and their light, a bright and quivering fire, cast a soothing golden-brown glow into her quarters at nightfall. Jésabel's apartment was in a very tall building, narrow and rickety, and the spiral staircase that wound its way up the quaint tower smelled sweetly of wax and pine. She had a lithe black cat named Elzéar, who at any moment would circle around her ankles, behind her back, or under her arms, so much so that she described him as a perpetual furry growth that purred.

I instantly liked Jésabel and her little world. For years our correspondence was abundant, trusting, a spark of joy in our shared old age. We were a mirror to each other, transposed into different milieus. We were like two rats in an experiment on the effects of the environment on a creature: she was the urban guinea pig, and I the forest specimen.

Her stationery was always blue-gray and mine, cream, and our letters criss-crossed in a regular ballet from one post office to the other. I would smile on seeing the mail carrier turning his car around in front of the House, because it meant he had just, unknowingly, delivered another moment of blissful reading into my letterbox. From two pages our letters expanded to four, then six. We never grew tired, we always had something to share, memories, moments of life, the color of the leaves in the trees. In this way I learned to tell my story, to bring my past back to life. It did me good to revive the childhood games we'd played—Klaus, Louisa, Harriett, the cousins, and I. I loved writing to her, as much for knowing I had an indefectible ally—whose existence I could sense, pulsing, so far from mine—as for the happy images that writing my memories evoked.

We never met. The thought never even crossed our minds: what would have been the point—we got along so well. I was afraid, just as she was, of being disappointed once again, as we'd been by all the strangers we'd allowed to enter our home, by the inevitable gap that always remained between them and our familiar world. I'd told her about Oktav, the importunate blot on the landscape of my garden, the inconsistency between my environment and him, the botched experiment, the sacrificed guinea pig.

One fine day she exceeded the maximum deadline of two weeks that we'd set ourselves, and no reply came. Initially I was a bit surprised, then saddened. I imagined she'd found another kindred spirit, an invasive neighbor who had broken the spell. I sent another letter. The only reply I got, three days later, was Elzéar in a carrier cage, and a brief letter from the notary which stated that in her will, Madame Jésabel Skatander had left me her cat and her books, and that everything else had been donated to the City.

I think Elzéar was very happy at the House. He immediately came to rub affectionately against me whenever I burst into tears while preparing the tea or watering the flowers. But Jésabel's furry growth died in turn, two years later. I was alone once more.

The remaining winters I spent at the House can be counted on the fingers of one hand. But they were bleak. From time to time people from the village came to make sure I was still alive. No doubt their intentions were good, but this drove me to the edge of a deep abyss, with death groaning at the bottom. I felt vulnerable and old. It was last winter that persuaded me to leave for this retirement home. My income was being eaten away by years of maintaining the House, of buying canned food at the grocery store, of sending letters to nieces and nephews on their birthdays, and this all made the winters harder and harder to bear. I had to resort to the services of a lumberjack to chop my firewood. It was expensive. So I was sparing with my logs, and the hearth was often cold. I'd had a space heater installed in the bedroom with the twin beds, so that neither Harriett's ghost nor I would be cold during the night. I thought I'd seen her shivering in silence one night, and it had broken my heart. The heater sufficed for the room, but the bathroom with its green tiles was more freezing than ever, the wind was once again seeping through the loose window joints. It was taking me forever to go down the stairs. My entire body was painful, dried out, and cold.

In the spring I decided to sell the House to the municipality in return for a life annuity, and I had them sign a contract which stipulated that nothing would be changed, that no one would live there, and that they would put a large padlock on the gate. I wanted to let the House rot. Let it fall apart, collapse inward on itself, like an exhausted horse folding on its legs, foam on its flanks. I wanted it to die from my departure, and wait for me to come and haunt it with all the other ghosts of my family, once death came for me.

Spring

Spring is beautiful at the House nevertheless. It never changes. Harriett and I wait for it every year, in the quivering of cold air. At first, our skin sips timidly at the new April sunshine, not daring to believe too boldly, still frozen from the marbled light of the long winter. Holding a strand of hair before our eyes, we inspect bright motes of low-angling sun dancing along our curls. It's still a bit chilly, so we hurry back indoors, stopping to wipe our feet, because the porch is wet from the brief morning rain. Then we look out the kitchen window to see how the gentle warmth is gradually reviving the moss in the orchard, and the blanket of blue grass in the sleeping garden. It's been getting warmer for a few days, a week, we leave our great-grandmother's sweaters on the back of a chair and they hang there, shuddering, their long sleeves dangling onto the tiled floor and dipping into the warm honey of sunlight. We stretch like lazy cats slipping out of their nap, happy as tightrope walkers unwinding in the golden hour of a new zenith. We can sense that something is happening, we listen as the birds return to the trees, gradually re-populating all the motionless world of treetops and skies. Louisa has regained some color, her skin taking on the lovely complexion of a delicate flower; she is blossoming in the hope of renewal. Petite Mère fears there will be frost, Petit Père calls the gardener for the first mowing of the year. The routine resumes. Day by day we keep an eye on the branches as they become heavy with buds, still green, while the sky is a blur of drifting pollen. We're already dreaming of those light dresses we'll soon be taking from the wardrobe, surely, now that the sun has arrived.

But April has always been a very disappointing month: for one week of overwhelming heat, we are immediately doused with curtains of freezing rain that seem never-ending, and once again we despair, with the irrational fear that winter is about to start all over again and summer will be nipped in the bud. On spring evenings, the soft light of the last fires in the hearth trembles as it is reflected in the rain-lashed window. We see the apple trees twisting in the blustery wind, their image distorted by the liquid scales undulating along the window pane. Harriett rests her chin on her fist, and sighs deeply in the half-light of the salon, because it's Louisa's turn to play and she always takes too long before arranging her word on the board. "It's not complicated, Louisa, even I can do it and I'm only in primary school," Harriett complains, curling up in her armchair. Klaus pinches her cheek, she screams, I laugh; Petit Père scolds us from his study. Petite Mère sweeps through the room, her shadow gliding past the hearth for a brief instant, blocking the light. "And besides, I can't see a thing!" Louisa grumbles. "You'll need glasses soon," says Klaus, mischievously. "No, never! I'd sooner die," she gasps with terror, wide-eyed, fluttering a long curl of eyelash. "Let's not take all day about it," says Harriett, exasperated. But in fact, we always took at least three hours.

I actually liked rainy evenings. We could hear the raindrops beating against the glass, our heads nestled comfortably on our pillows, and hands tucked in armpits, under the duvet, there where it was warmest, where the body maintained its own warmth like a good little organic fireplace. "Listen to the rain," I murmured, when Harriett asked me if I was asleep. So she fell silent and listened. How good it felt to be inside, in the warm, when everything was cracking and streaming outside, where a strong nocturnal wind was blowing with all its force against the wooden structure of the House. But the House was always stronger, it creaked and moaned from cellar to attic, a valiant ship with a warm hold, all its timbers shivering, its portholes rattling with the effort. Sometimes a faint anxiety went through me when the howling of the heavens was joined by the cries of the roof beams two floors above our little room. Then it felt like the wind was about to smash its fist through the shutters, and burst through our cottony cocoon, the silence of the corridors, the half-open doors in the sleeping House. Harriett was already asleep, and I told myself that if the wind broke in, I'd leap out of bed and run to cover her, to take the brunt of the onslaught of blades of rain, millions of little knives on our skin. I shivered in my sheets, and then, as if by magic, the wind dropped and my skin was warm through my cotton pajamas. I wiggled my legs under the blankets, in complete darkness, and I listened to the comforting rubbing of my calves against the sheet. I was alive. I was in my bed, every limb responded the way it should to my command. I tried different rhythms, with a delightful sensation of childish power, of mastering my own body, enchanted by my coordination, one-two, one-two, one-two-three, one-two-three . . . And suddenly from the next bed came a rubbing sound that was in step with mine, two more little calves joining the rhythm, and we giggled in the dark, having each other guess songs by hammering our heels on the mattress.

Age weighs on a person's limbs, like a gloomy late afternoon. There's a taste of old, metallic tea on the tongue, a furry tongue all cozy behind lips sealed with pain. At least the laundry smells good here, and my shirt collars are neatly ironed, nice and stiff against the skin on my neck, with that cheering crispness that clean clothes have. My hands are swollen with veins on the faded fabric of my nightgown. Little white flowers against a pale green background. Cotton that's clean and fresh, blue clouds in a white sky. Everything is backwards. They do everything for me, they wash my bed linen, it vanishes, they return it folded and ironed, with a pleasant voice waiting for thanks, and so you say thank you to the caregiver, because she cares and gives. There's nothing she can do if we cry a little on seeing that impersonal bed linen covering us.

We had lovely sheets, at the House, monogrammed, so we knew right away whose bed they clothed. They were all white, an inimitable white, and it was only the embroidered letters that enabled us to differentiate them. The sheets were always a source of teasing quarrels among Petit Père, Aunt Hilde, and Uncle Bertie, when they came to visit, before. Petit Père insisted on giving them the same bed linen they'd grown up in, respectively, with their initials embroidered on it. Hilde always exclaimed, "You keep these old things?" "We've had the same napkins since we were children, so we're keeping them," grumbled Petit Père, vexed that his sister and brother were not as attached to tradition as he was.

Petit Père told us that for each birth, the eldest woman in the family would embroider the infant's initials on a set of sheets which would stay with them their whole life long. The art of monogramming, the art of the ritual, a pair of sheets that followed us like a burden. *I. A.* in emerald green for my set. Isadora Aberfletch. It's strange how that color, which my grandmother had arbitrarily assigned to me two days after my birth, has stayed with me all through life and ended up defining my esthetic tastes. When I would lie on my stomach reading in bed, I dreamily stroked those letters, with the downstrokes and upstrokes of the fine capital letters solidly attached to the white sheet, a stream of emerald set against a strand of sand. *I. A.* I murmured the two letters that sounded like a fierce war cry, and I loved it. I felt predestined to fight. I read my future in the embroidered letters, I grew attached to the slightest irregularity in the thread, and I told myself that it corresponded to some future unpleasantness. I tried to determine the age at which this irregularity would befall me, depending on where on the letter it was located. On the I: early in life; on the A: closer to the end. I don't have those sheets anymore, I wasn't allowed to bring them here. In the end, I don't know whether the letters were right.

One of my favorite moments in spring was the Great House Cleaning. I experienced the same frenzy as in the days of painting in summer. It was the same purity of the immaculate, the same dizzying bedazzlement, sheets flapping and billowing in the good sunlight full of pollen and scents, in the garden. We played between the sheets as they hung on their lines, we scared each other by disappearing behind the damp sails of a ship tossing under an azure sky. A cool shadow was cast by the drying sheets, and they exhaled the sweet, comforting smell of family laundry. Harriett and I dried off nearby, sprawled in the grass that was still cold in the first spring sun. Blue sky, white sheets, deep green grass on the lawn strengthened by the recent melting of the snows, everything intoxicating and warming our little bodies. Then suddenly the damp from the lawn would grab us by the throat—or was it the pollen-rich breeze that was tickling our nostrils? And then we'd hurry into the House like a flutter of sparrows, bringing with us tiny insects in our hair, which we then discovered, disgusted, during the evening brush. When the floors shone with soapy water, Petite Mère shouted at us to be careful not to walk in the rooms she'd just mopped, so we hugged the walls like Sioux Indians, laughing provocatively when we lost our balance and a foot landed clumsily on a spot that was still wet.

Petite Mère was always restrained, always discreet, but she narrowly avoided the status of the useless, decorative wife thanks to the independence required by her art, which made her spend a great deal of time alone in her studio on the veranda, or trekking around the property at all times of day. We hardly ever ran into her, she was relatively absent, somewhat diluted, like a bucolic watercolor. She resembled those pale, gentle women so lauded by poets, with large, faded eyes. Louisa was a much headier version of Petite Mère, her charm more formidable. As for Harriett and me, we were afraid not only of becoming self-effacing the way she was, but also of never being able to resemble her. Very early on, we'd become resigned. I realized I wanted neither to be anyone's muse, nor to be sung and placed on a pedestal; just barely loved. I didn't care, particularly as a child. I recall that Petite Mère already annoyed me, at the time; her sweetness irritated me and at the same time calmed me down, it was both a stimulus and a balm. Today I acknowledge that salutary self-effacement of hers, which was the warranty of our freedom. We would never have been so independent if we had not, from the start, been so terrified by her own evanescence.

In the spring, she turned to painting flowers again. And although she knew their every nuance and contour by heart, she needed to have them there before her eyes, the shedding petals of young primroses, the tender porcelain forget-me-nots frothing under the apple trees. We made a point of honor of providing her with her bouquets, and every morning she'd put in her order; for this evening I'd like blues; for this evening I'd like nuances of yellow, white, and pink. As we strolled around we'd pick the flowers she requested. Thus, our walks were quietly accompanied by Petite Mère's voice describing her desired bouquet. We brought it to her toward the end of the afternoon, and she painted until late at night, because she liked the glow from the hearth that obliged her to brighten her colors, or so she said. "My blues are dull when I paint by daylight." In the morning, on the veranda, on the easel haloed in dawn light, we would find a new painting, our bouquet on canvas. The real flowers were in a vase on the kitchen table. Every spring, the House filled with bouquets as the days went by. The bouquets from the previous days would make their way upstairs, to decorate bedside tables, the rim of a bathtub, a corner by the window. The whole House was in bloom, little touches of color disseminated through every room. We would find petals in our sheets, or under furniture, sometimes weeks later, when they'd dried and turned amber like the wings of a dead butterfly.

Sometimes, although this was rarer, Petite Mère wanted to paint Louisa. She had a springtime face, she said. Harriett and I did not take offense. We would have hated to pose for hours, and we knew our sister was the prettiest. And so we set about transforming Louisa into a nymph. We ran into the garden, and came back with our arms full of a harvest of corollas, which we poured onto the floor of the veranda—peonies, roses, daisies, and bindweed. The veranda filled with the smell of the flowers' poison, and a languor came over us as we stood around Louisa, sticking delicate petals into her curls. She hardly quivered, so preoccupied was she with appearing graceful. Petite Mère smiled at her and caressed her cheek with the brush, then she tickled our ears as we went by, and it made us laugh all the way up to our room. We left them to their work, and we went to play on our own, or to bother Klaus while he was reading or practicing the trumpet. When the picture was finished, Louisa reappeared, her gaze tired and her limbs numb, and she kept her crown of flowers on her head like a diadem. She glided in her dressing gown toward the mirror to admire herself like that, a slender red-cheeked wood fairy.

As a child, Louisa used to draw. We'd run to tell her something, or invite her to play, but then we'd stop, as if held back, at the entrance to her room. She was bent over her desk by the big window that let in the sleepy afternoon light. With her elbow held to one side, as if to take her momentum, the other hand holding the sheet of paper on the edge of the table, she was drawing elegant women and invented witches.

I liked seeing her like that, busy, febrile, how she didn't hear us when we called out to her. In moments like that she seemed to withdraw from the stage of the world, where ordinarily she performed her graceful ballet, in order to lose herself backstage in the delight of drifting in a place where we could not follow.

Petite Mère and Petit Père were ecstatic when they saw her drawings, and we loved them, too. She portrayed scenes inspired by the games we used to play, or would play in the future. This imagination, I realize now, was something we all shared—Harriett, Louisa, Klaus, and I. There were images and characters inspired by the fairytales we'd been told as children, stories of kings and bears, of witches and warriors, halfway between a jungle exoticism and a fairyland of ice.

It's painful to think that, in the end, Louisa was no different from us, basically, although we often thought that, among the siblings, she was the outsider. Now I can see that, imperceptibly, we were sisters, without it being too obvious, almost secretly. She is absent from many of my memories. What was she doing when Harriett and I were running through the garden in the spring? Did she find it beautiful, the way we did? She probably also went for walks, but more slowly, seeking other things we were not aware of, in the opulence of fresh-blown flowers.

Spring was the time when once again we took an interest in the earth. Suddenly our gazes fell toward our feet as they sank into the young grass. All at once the horizon was lower down; we spent all our time crouching down by flower beds dotted with young shoots, or among the swarming roots of the fruit trees, or over the tall stalks infested with aphids. We'd roll a bud between our fingers, astonished by its perfect consistency, solid and soft like the plump little flesh of a baby's finger. We could feel the vigorous blades of grass tickling our ankles; the warm May wind filled our clothes, disheveled from running. We were completely at one with the world; the self became an empty House opened to the four winds, where wide flat ripples of sunlight played. We rediscovered the infinitely small. We could squat down for an entire hour at the foot of the porch where we knew an ant colony was busier than ever, year after year. We hunted for red bugs, those limping policemen that went around two by two, stuck together, monstrous couples losing themselves among the tangled roots of bushes. Harriett looked out for them more than anyone, and took great pleasure in forcing them, with a twig, to change their itinerary. Relentlessly she'd place sudden obstacles in their path—pebbles, leaves, her implacable foot; she harpooned them, harassed them, numbed them. Her eyes shone with wild delight when, hitting them with a twig, she managed to drive them apart in the midst of impregnation; she watched as their bellies swollen with mysterious life burst under the slow pressure of her branch. The red carapace was crushed in its precious juice, and we swore, half-repulsed, half-fascinated, that we would never get pregnant if it meant having a belly filled like that with whitish slime.

And we continued to search, digging in every corner of the garden, looking under every stone, in every flower bed, for a new colony to torture. This meant massacres of anthills, the pillaging of spiderwebs, an absolutely gratuitous and enchanting vandalizing of the living. I was afraid, however, that once night had fallen the insects might come and seek revenge, that while we were asleep they would form a column and march straight into our warm, half-open mouths. They were terrifying in number, their little legs twitching with jolts of pain. I even imagined the cries they gave inside, in a language of suffering insects, and this thought tormented my mind. I tugged Harriett by the arm to make her stop. She backed away, with a shrug of her shoulders and a spiteful gaze.

I remember clearly that the fever of propagation, with its dampness of spring impregnation, was repulsive to me. I was ill at ease when the village cats meowed their guts out, when the birds chased each other with a febrile rustling of their wings.

I found them brusque, they startled me, I ran at them to drive them away. When I was an adolescent, the springtime hammered me with its anvil of love: I felt crushed. Only with disgust did I let the seal leave its imprint. I couldn't take it anymore, all that lubricious saturation around me, I was too young, I didn't understand. This triumph of obscene burgeoning, the pungent whiff of pollen, the untimely swarming of bees all plunged me into a springtime malaise that I felt all through part of my adolescence.

And then, as if by magic, I noticed that I was not just a mind in a functional body that served to run or dance. I was part of an organic whole, and there was nothing shameful about it. I destroyed the sacred aura surrounding the power of desire and then, very gradually, that power opened out. I agreed to desire. I told myself I would be the most charming of lovers. I began my love affair with Oktav at the age of eighteen. It was serious, I even brought him to the House once, at the end of a month of May. At the time it was the most important step I could have taken. But on seeing him out of his usual habitat in the City, superimposed upon my garden and my House, an invasive blot on the landscape, I understood we would not end up together. In my beloved countryside he stood out like a sore thumb. He could not be part of it, despite his deep, beautiful eyes, despite the light that spiked the blond down on his earlobes with white.

It was four years later that I turned down his proposal, that famous winter. The way he clashed, unconsciously, with my nest and my forest, was the first of a long suite of discrepancies and diverging opinions. There was nothing we wanted together. Each of us wanted to force the other to marry his or her own future, because we saw only too well that they did not match, and would never match.

I often think back on that time, in spite of everything. There are recurring memories that I summon—the white wood of the House, Harriett's little hand, the fire crackling, the warm tiles in the kitchen when the jam is bubbling in the pot. As for the memory of Oktav, it recurs without warning, always rather painfully. No matter how much I loved my solitude I have never, since that time, loved anyone the way I loved Oktav. He remains my point of reference, to whom I later compared all my relationships. Above all I loved the way he would laugh and show his teeth, briefly; he was incredibly luminous. To watch him laugh was to grasp, fleetingly, a part of his being that he hid from the world the rest of the time. Inside, he was clear, with the clarity of a feast day, the clarity of a restaurant in evening light, resonant with soft, delicate laughter amid the clatter of cutlery.

And yet I said no, when he asked me to marry him, I said no and I knew how much it would shatter us both. I watched with resignation as the fracture parted his lips. I didn't kiss him to close it. I let him crack under the weight of that huge No.

Louisa got married the following year. It was her wedding that made me love spring again. While it wasn't summer, it brought all the family together; it triumphed over the hundreds of kilometers that had torn us apart, to fuse us together under the blue May sky.

I kept the photos we took that day. In the box under the television, there's a big brown album with a gilt binding. I'll leaf through it later, but I don't really need to. I can see it all, still.

Louisa and Gallead in sky blue, powdered with silver, as splendid as kings, clutching each other's arm to keep from slipping on the grass, which was still saturated with the previous day's rain. Enormous sprays of white flowers were strewn along the path to the orchard where we'd erected the arch of their union among the lettuces. Louisa's hair was perfectly braided, beautiful, long, thick blonde ribbons twisted on her peachy neck. And everyone wore a radiant expression, squinting slightly in the dazzling sunlight, hands joined as if to pray and applaud in a single gesture, in the intertwining of the Vow and cries of Bravo! There was the effervescence of the banquet, the congratulations tossed out in a crafty voice by Amelia and Magda, neither of whom were very well-married, to a pair of nice boys. Gazes look skyward as a white train of mackerel sky enters the blue; if it rains we'll have to run for it, but the clouds go by, and everything is fizzing again. The tinkling of cutlery on the white plates is gentle and restrained.

It was Louisa and at the same time it wasn't Louisa. She had the smile of a bride, rendered rather apologetic by ceremonial happiness. Gallead was one of those men who succeed at everything, is handsome as a god, has a good position, charms the parents, and is polite and refined. I must have been jealous of Louisa for a second or two, the time of a pang in my heart, then my eyes met my sister's gaze, already resigned; on her finger a delicate diamond shone under that spring sky, while petals were thrown in the air like clods of earth after a shell explosion. I sensed she would not be happy.

When a taxi pulled up by the porch of the House, many years later, and I saw her from the window of the study take her son's hand, holding back her tears, a secret joy came over me. The House would be repopulated, as it was meant to be. It was calling its inhabitants back to its walls, it was opening its doors again to take them in and make them better. I did my best to ensure that everything would be different from the last summer we'd seen each other, when my outburst in the attic had scattered the last fragments of our family like a flight of ravens. I thought, naïvely, that Louisa would stay forever this time, that she had understood that, out there, men are cruel and when the cobblestones are wet the City is truly ugly.

And so Louisa had come back. I took her in with all the gentleness she required. I turned to Petite Mère's gracious, measured gestures for inspiration; they came back to me almost spontaneously in my sudden role as caregiver. Louisa was truly suffering. Her mind could come up with nothing but thoughts of wool and dreams of stone, gray and heavy. Gallead was not cut out for family life. He'd decided, at the dawn of his fortieth year, that he'd rather resume his life as a bachelor. It was almost too much of a foregone conclusion to seem convincing. Kurt had become a lively, athletic boy, something of an *enfant terrible*, dark and brooding. He reminded me of Klaus when little, but a Klaus who'd known great unhappiness and had therefore taken a more tortuous path. Kurt was a considerate boy, and he helped me throughout their stay at the House, with every task the garden required during that sweet, mild spring. Kurt picked and ran and spun about, and I ran with him, almost as if I were the same age. At the time I was just over thirty-five, but this boy no longer viewed me as a grownup, because I wasn't like the other grownups he knew, who were glum and quarrelsome. This gave me a certain sense of pride. It was as if he had forgotten the aunt he'd known all those summer ago, the woman about whom they must have said so many nasty things, who suddenly blew up over an open trunk. Because of the divorce, his parents had proven more disappointing, belittling themselves so much more than they belittled others when they stood hurling insults in front of the boy. He'd seen too much passion, thus I offered him my own dis-passion, my lack of brilliance, my haven out of time where we could flit through the monotony of days like fairies that were creatures of habit.

I tried my best not to reproduce the mistakes I'd made that last summer when everyone left without saying a word. Kurt's refreshing attitude was precious to me, and I made an effort not to stop him going to the attic. I tried not to see him as having Harriett's curly little head, or watch him play among the clotheslines hung with sheets. But Louisa was becoming increasingly tense, precisely, I think, because of my efforts. Despite myself, I still betrayed the odd gesture of annoyance. One evening, once Kurt had gone to bed, she said she would have liked to forgive me for my violence. At that precise moment, she added something that confirmed everything I'd felt as a child, confusedly, about my older sister. She confessed that she'd never felt she belonged to this family, to this House. That she'd always been left on the sidelines of our games, and had felt confined by the stifling cocoon, so far from everything. She'd always wanted to leave, and she insulted me terribly by evoking, there before me, everything she hated about the rest of us. She murmured that I lived an unhealthy life, clinging as I did to the past, clinging to a childhood I'd idealized. Once she'd started she couldn't stop, coming out with the most horrible things: she said that Petite Mère had never been happy with Petit Père, that this House had been an ordeal for her, a crushing responsibility. I thought Louisa had finished, but then she began spitting more venom: "Petite Mère never had her initials embroidered on her bed linen; she had the plain white napkins the wives were given. The House weighed on her like the slab of a tombstone, she was suffocating under all the terrible pressure on her womb, there, a womb twisted with the fear of ruin, the fear of death. Petite Mère had her brats all right, and she scrubbed her floors, you owe them to her, your clean floors and your transparent windows. You think she was gentle, she smelled sweetly of soap? She painted flowers, did she? But if you only knew the violence with which she painted, you stupid girl, she pinned all the chopped-off heads of bleeding corollas to the canvas . . . didn't you know that? Oh go on, of course you did, you knew, you were just too selfish, too clueless, too happy. She had terrible migraines, she got them the minute she opened her eyes in the morning, as a child I could already hear her wringing the sheets in the next room. Needles in her skull, Isadora, just think, she could feel it eating away at her eyelids, and you, and Harriett, you were downstairs screaming, playing your games that were ever noisier, ever more boisterous. Your little feet running back and forth, endlessly running, and Petite Mère moaning, so I had to get up not to hear any more of it. She couldn't do anything, couldn't be anywhere but here, she was a stranger in her husband's family House, don't you see, she was padlocked to him, and to everyone else. And you never even went to see her, at the end . . . " Louisa had calmed down, had collapsed into an armchair. I was on my knees begging her to stop. For a few minutes she watched as I wept, stunned with sorrow. And then exhausted and bitter, all she murmured was that Petite Mère, without knowing it, had married into a cursed lineage of master builders, a dynasty of façades to be repainted every year.

That evening, Louisa had unveiled an entire world I didn't want to understand, a tainted vision of everything I loved. Over the last five years we'd lived through the deaths, one after the other, of our mother, our father, and our little sister. She accused me of stealing her grief from her, of stealing her childhood, by living here alone, unchanged, in the place we'd grown up. I understood a lot of things, although I was extremely angry with her. I tried to defend myself, she was blowing everything out of proportion, that much was certain, exaggerating people's unhappiness just to hurt me, to destroy our family.

Later, in my bed, I came to see that Louisa was right, and that to spare me she must have kept all that to herself for years. I understood that everything she'd done—constantly avoiding us, leaving the House so young, not telling me how much Petite Mère had suffered—had been done principally for herself, but also, to some extent, for me. She sensed that, sooner or later, she'd be obliged to destroy the lie of happiness; it enraged her to see me like this, full of illusions, when she was so much closer to the truth. It was just that for me, grief meant all sorts of strange whims that were driven and maintained by the solitude of my hideaway, rotten with nostalgia, in the middle of our childhood trees. She had no business dragging me into her disgust regarding the family, into her flight from the past. We have never operated in the same way. When she left, I stayed, stubbornly. I don't know why I'm like this, why I perpetually want to relive everything. Staying was my way to resist obliteration, oblivion.

Basically, in my life there was only one tragedy. I would give everything to have Harriett back again.

I gave
everything.

Louisa went away again just before the end of the summer, taking Kurt with her. He didn't even cry. Once again I'd become the strange aunt living as a recluse in that cool big House of hers. Our evening of revelations left Louisa and me not angry but very sad. As they were leaving we stood with our arms around each other for a long time. She seemed to be saying, little sister, I forgive you for needing your lies. We had not hugged each other like that in a long time. Among themselves, grownups don't cuddle, even if they love one another. We reserve our embraces for lovers or husbands, and cuddles for little children. For everyone else, a strange modesty takes hold, an organic distance. But that hug on the porch, with Louisa, was necessary. We should never stop showing affection, among brothers and sisters.

In November I heard that she was going to re-marry, a certain Andrew, a colleague of Gallead's. The wedding was held in the winter, in a warm greenhouse in the heart of the City's botanical garden, rented for the occasion. I decided not to attend, and sent a wreath woven with holly from our woods.

I gradually grew accustomed to the idea that, for the others, the House was no more than an interlude. For them the House had something of a curse on it, heavy with sorrow, with frozen memories. I also understood that now only Klaus, Louisa, and I were left, and that they didn't see the House the way I did. It took a lot out of them, emotionally, to come back, whereas I very much enjoyed feeling the reassuring weight of the past on my shoulders. There was a presence there with me.

Solitude, in springtime, is both sweeter and more bitter than solitude during other seasons. Animals emerge from their winter quarters with a desire to see their own kind again, to mix their breath with the reunited herd which, round with new pregnancies, is making its way, sniffling and snorting, toward the great plains of pastureland. I had a more enduring desire to see my kin again, too. Because the secret joy of flowers growing had become more difficult for me without Harriett, and the insects fluttering from corolla to corolla made me even more acutely aware of how life would not be starting over for her. Flowers, plants, moss, insects, all the little world so dear to Harriett, had seemed futile to me since her death. There was no point in re-flowering.

Then, progressively, the first weeks of spring, that false spring when snow can still fall, inevitably gave way to the golden months of May and June, those months of good warm air, plans, exaltation. Spring always took hold of me right toward the end. Now when I opened the shutters every morning, it was with joy that I saw the flowers, ever more resplendent in bright daylight. I went from room to room, window to window, letting the stream of sunlight and pollen sweep into the House. I would enter a room that was still shuttered, and leave it again flooded with light; the mahogany parquet shone beneath my dancing feet. The laundry dried well, quickly, no more the tedious hanging out, like in winter, of heavy wet sheets weighing coldly on lines stretched taut across the entrance hall. In spring, the laundry in its basket warmed in the morning sun as it waited to be hung, sheet upon sheet, dress upon dress, unfolded, shaken, laid over the line against the blue sky. This was outdoor laundry, the laundry we would take in on clear June days, basket on hip, when we knew it must be dry.

The House was a formidable reservoir of clothing, for every age, of every color; from cellar to attic wardrobes overflowed, enormous trunks were piled up, moaning painfully on their hinges. I have never needed or wanted to go into the City to go shopping. As a child I wore Louisa's hand-me-downs, which were still very pretty, of exquisite taste; even Klaus's old cast-offs, which I actually liked better because they were more appropriate for adventuring in the garden. As an adult all I had to do was rummage through each room: here I might find one of Petit Père's shirts, to pair with the pleated trousers that Great-Aunt Babel had received from a lover in the City sixty years earlier. I wanted for nothing, I wove my way through other people's stories and textiles with delight. I went from men's clothing to women's; from that of the distant to that of the dead. Full of wonder I pulled hangers from closets, and every wardrobe in every room had its treasures, its little follies: muslin gloves from the last century, Great-Aunt Babel's furs, of course; lightweight skirts, maternity garments—those shapeless undergarments, was that what my grandmother had worn when she was expecting my father? What doubt and terror and joy did she feel when her hands observed the roundness of her belly? Forgotten clothing, full of twigs, wadded up and abandoned in a closet; summer or vacation outfits, blouses I remember seeing the cousins wear when they were children. That straw hat: whose was that? I rolled the brim thoughtfully between my fingers, while every head in the family paraded through my thoughts. In that dress Aunt Hilde, as a young adolescent, must have felt quite beautiful as she looked in the mirror, and I felt beautiful in turn when I tried it on. What seemed strangest of all was when, a few years after Petite Mère died, I began to examine her wardrobe with curiosity, and before long I had found everything I might possibly ever need. We had ended up with the same body, and that was what struck me most. Sometimes, on getting a glimpse of my reflection in the kitchen window, I was startled, because I thought I could see my mother in the porcelain blue dress she wore in the spring. The same size, the same suppleness of the arms: I looked at myself, dumbfounded, dancing slowly in the transparency of the windowpane. I had become my mother, and I was preparing tea, then I headed out to the veranda, and slowly stirred the old paintbrushes in their jars. In the evening, it suddenly turned cool with nightfall, and I put on one of Petit Père's jackets. How strange, some of them smelled of Uncle Bertie's honey cigars, probably because they spent so much time talking together in the salon after dinner, those summers.

When I'd put all the clothes I'd worn that week out to dry on the laundry line, it was as if I weren't alone anymore, seeing them next to each other, hanging by their elbows: Petit Père's jackets, Petite Mère's dresses, one of Louisa's shawls, Klaus's shirts. Anybody who happened to walk past the garden would have said, on seeing such an array of laundry, a big family must live there. And yet I was alone, wearing these clothes, washing them, hanging them out to dry; alone.

But springtime knows no silence. It seemed as if all the fine nature vibrating around me was thinking and feeling. It seemed as if I had given birth to it. I kept a close eye on the seedlings, the shoots, the first fruit from the orchard, with an attentiveness that made me smile. I bent over the cabbages the way you bend over a crib. I spread the leaves as if they were the delicate netting filtering the light into a baby carriage.

I became a little girl again. Sitting on the grassy slope below the House, I made wreaths of flowers. I found a patch of grass strewn with daisies, and spread my skirts wide over my legs, pricked by blades of grass. I picked the most beautiful flowers around me, I was a giant raiding the stone cottages of a tiny human village with my big fist. Then I attached all the flowers together, murderously using the stem to spear each yellow, welcoming heart, all powdery with pollen. The stems grew white with the tight knots I made, it was easier to do so as an adult than as a child. I squinted in the flow of yellow light, which whitened my lowered lashes. I was forty, then suddenly I was ten. Once the wreath was finished, it was only for me, would fit only my brow, but in my thoughts I pictured Louisa and Harriett adjusting similar crowns on their heads, warm with sunlight. Louisa, the fairy of flowered crowns, the queen of this garden: in the evening on the phone I told her that I'd been thinking of her while making my wreath, I told her how she'd always known how to choose the loveliest of daisies, and to make the sturdiest knots. She replied that she didn't really remember, and besides, she wouldn't know how to make them anymore.

But Harriett would have remembered, she would have enjoyed talking, together, about our games, on the telephone. Above all she would have been with me in the spring, in the House. Even when we were in our sixties we would have made wreaths of flowers. We would have spoken about all and sundry, our words coming easily, without thinking, petal by petal. We would have had lovers, no doubt, male or female, and we could have talked and laughed like two sisters still growing up and moving from children's games on to women's secrets.

But since I didn't have a sister with me, I spoke to no one. There was no one I liked. For me to meet someone, he would have had to come up to the front gate.

All things considered, it was rather a bit of a miracle that took place, initially disguised as a curse, when one spring, Klaus called to inform me that he was hoping, with his big band, to compose a jazz album that a record company had been urging him to produce. Initially this news seemed to concern me only remotely, then he added that he'd be coming that very week with his band, and their instruments and trunks, to the House. You understand, dear little sister, the House has always inspired me, and it's so good to be there in the spring. Our ideas will flow freely, he added, they'll come to us like a cat brushing quickly against its master's legs. Basically, he was in need of hospitality for a whole slew of musicians, and for several weeks. At first, in a bit of a panic, I refused, sensing that this would cause a great disturbance, a terrible inconvenience, of raucous men and trumpets blasting at dawn and thumping steps on the aging floorboards. Klaus cheerfully reassured me, and promised he'd keep a tight rein on his henchmen. In his opinion, my fears were ridiculous. He was right, because it turned out that reality far exceeded my worst expectations.

The Titus Transpolar Timorius Band already enjoyed a certain renown by the time they all turned up at the entrance to the House with a great fanfare of car horns, shouts, grunts, and aftershave. This was my brother's company for his time off between two conductor's tailcoats, a time when he went slumming at night in jazz clubs with his trumpet at the ready. Trailing behind him was a gang of friends gleaned from the various orchestras he'd once conducted, or musicians he'd known since his student days. This merry company of artists in their fifties were beginning to gain a quite serious reputation on the global avant-garde stage, and this new album would hopefully crown their success with unanimous critical acclaim. It was in this state of mind that the twelve members of the Titus Transpolar Timorius Band—two tubas, three trombones, four trumpets, one double bass, and two percussionists—arranged their well-polished shoes in a row in the entrance hall, at my bidding.

The garden was in full flower, the birds were chirping with all the insouciance of their brand new nests. The second evening, a little bar piano they'd had delivered during the day was accidentally knocked over by a trombonist and a trumpet player, crushing my bed of lilac hydrangeas. One week later, an arm chair in the salon, fortunately not my favorite one, was splattered with whisky during a lively discussion about the tempo of a particular piece. In the course of the three months they spent at the House that year, I lost, in all, one flower bed, one armchair, four glasses, two plates, and half an eardrum, because from morning to night there was an excessive cascade of virtuoso brass, snare drum solos, and human roars that sounded as if they were coming from a gargantuan elephant. When I was trying to read in the garden there came, all at the same time, an outpouring of sharp notes from one window, the banging of cymbals from another, a chant of trombones from the skylight in the attic, and an inane melody blasting the veranda, all of which caused me to let go of my book. There was clear laughter, and hearty laughter, and laughter that was hoarse from honey cigars—they'd found a box in Uncle Bertie's usual room. They marched around with constant bursts of brass from their lips; musical scores were scattered everywhere, on every piece of furniture, in the kitchen, even in the bathtub. On opening my wardrobe one morning I found a tambourine in my underwear, and I could hear peals of laughter from the other side of the door, from some idiot or other. Towels gathered, like in the grand old days when the family filled the House, to dry indiscriminately on banisters, on door handles, on backs of chairs. All this brood of men under my roof, this constant commotion of jovial lads, late adolescents, struck me as both utterly unbearable and the most thrilling experience ever.

Because I myself, in all this, would walk around the busy rooms feeling a bit coquettish, and they greeted me like a queen, and rushed to help with the daily chores. For the most part they were not boors, and if they saw me go by outdoors with a spade in hand they would leave their practice and run to help me in the garden. It was like having an entire pack of brothers. Klaus was charming, funny, and warm, as always, and he was careful to include me in their world. He always saved a seat for me near him at the table, and he would expeditiously dispatch one of his friends to do the shopping, or prepare the meal, or set the table. This entire little summer camp made me feel more alive than ever, my blood hurtling, racing furiously through my veins. I awoke to the aroma of coffee, and I would lie there, restless, with a big smile on my face, thinking, could it be that I was eight years old, and downstairs the grownups were making breakfast, and then Harriett and I would open the shutters and go tearing down to the kitchen into floods of light to wolf down our tartines? The empty little bed basking in the sun's rays next to me no longer seemed so sad, because on seeing it, my daydreaming stopped, but made way for a reality that was just as sweet. I was a woman, not a girl. My skin was warm, my hips were round, and my breasts still firm, and I knew that when I went downstairs I would be greeted by amusing, attentive men who respected me. I also knew that Markus fancied me, and I fancied him.

Markus was one of the reasons that this cohabitation was so pleasant. An absolutely charming trombonist, to whom I was genuinely attracted. A gentle fire warmed my ribs when I saw him standing in the salon, speaking animatedly. We were discreet, but it was glorious all the same to embrace in secret, in all the most unlikely places around the House and the garden, well away from all the others. Breathless, laughing, fearful of discovery at any moment. We were absolutely incognito, but when our gazes met across the dinner table, we could not help but smile at the organic secret that bound us, unbeknownst to all.

When they left, Klaus said quickly, with a laugh, that he'd have liked for me to find a lover among his friends, because they were the only people he'd gladly have as brothers-in-law, and deep within I felt happy, and full of mirth.

The summer was particularly hard to take, after they'd gone. I'd grown used to their noise, their smell, their instruments all over the House, their bouquets of wildflowers placed on the table, their big fists drumming on the doors, "Jermie, are you in there?" "Is the toilet occupied?" "Roh, come on, play Barmus, you're not funny." The album came out in September, for the new musical season, and was a huge success. Some of the tracks even became standards, including the one they'd entitled "Isadora," to thank me. Yes, the famous "Isadora," which is played nowadays in all the good, and less good, jazz clubs the world over, was dedicated to me. It is one of the most beautiful gifts I've ever received. Moreover, in the original version, Markus plays the solo. He'd insisted on it, Klaus said.

Springtime, in my fifties, and even my sixties, was very gentle. As if reassured that it had made it through the winter, my body felt the rebirth of things with even greater gratitude and wonder. In the morning I would go out through the veranda and stretch in the sunlight, feeling full to bursting with my own self. I was glad of the solidity of my mature body, as if I were physically moored to my land. I would head off for a walk in the woods, with a thick sweater over my shoulders, which became progressively useless as I got warm in the new sun filtering through the blue branches. Sometimes I went deep into the forest, and ran my hands over some of the rough tree trunks, and the veins of the bark against my ageing palms seemed to throb with tenderness. The full awareness of my good fortune, the full measure of what I owned, everything I thought I might experience until my death filled me with indescribable joy. I sometimes took a detour by the lake. At the end of winter it was even dirtier than usual, with dead branches intertwined in black hoops over the russet water.

The surface of water has always hypnotized me. The lake water may well have been as opaque as a tomb, I still plunged my gaze into it, and it seemed to me that the depths were now clear, that through a particular connection with this lake, so similar to my iris, everything that was happening in the murky shadows of the water was visible to me. I could sense the huge earth-colored carps moving through silent strata, rippling the dense water like a pool of satin. I could sense the throbbing of the lively little fish, panicking in disarray in the tall grasses by the lake shore. My eyes, filled in this way with lake water, overflowed with awareness and understanding; as I leaned attentively over the shimmer of the depths I kept watch, with eye-piercing intensity, over the confused shadows below the ripples. It was like a secret revealed to me alone, for a brief instant, an intimate connection between surface and lake bed, and I was the ferryman. Then everything tipped over, upside down, and I was at the bottom of the lake, my eyes struggling to see through to the sky, to the light and the willows. I floated under the brown water and saw my surface self leaning blurrily toward my aquatic self. Suddenly a movement in the woods broke the spell, and the lake was restored to its green opacity.

Everything instantly made sense again—the trees were back in their place, in a circle around the lake. I looked at my boots, they'd taken on a bit of water, at the toes, because the sole was coming loose. I must have put my foot in the lake while I was gazing at it. Suddenly I began to shiver, a childish fear had returned, that of being hypnotized by the lake and drawn to the bottom, like in those legends where something is shining at the heart of the water, and the fascinated hero is drowned. I felt a bit silly in my wet socks, standing by my dirty lake where probably only very ugly fish swam, their gills full of sand.

I went back to the House. I knew the way by heart, I hardly ever paid attention to the curve of the path. Eventually I came out onto the lawn, and the House rose up huge and white before me in the garden. My stride lengthened, all I could think of now was taking off my boots and drying my socks by the fire, with a steaming cup. In moments like that, when I had just lost myself in the outdoors, I didn't stop to look at the House. I thought only of what it contained: kitchen, teapot, fireplace, slippers. I stopped looking up, on crossing the lawn. I regret it, now. I should have always gazed up at the House when I emerged from the woods, just as when, as a child, I was dazzled by its façade shining in the sun. One should always make an effort to see familiar things, to really see them. One should visit one's own palace with all the astonishment of a foreign ambassador.

I should have cherished it better, that private habitat each of us occupies all our life, and I'm no longer referring to the House but to the body, which you see only from above, or facing you, unless you're good at self-contortion. You'll never see your own body the way others see it; if you're curious, you'll always look avidly at photographs where you appear. So that's what I look like, you'll say to yourself, scrutinizing your fixed image. If the photographs captured you in the process of closing your eyes, or speaking, or making a clumsy gesture, if you're blurry, then the image you take away will be deeply disappointing; it's a missed opportunity to appreciate oneself, to know oneself. You look down at yourself and you see your breasts on your belly, the bulge of your abdomen, which used to swell on the days you had your period, and which has swollen for good now. Below that your thighs stand out, plump, smooth, and white, hiding your calves. The tips of your feet emerge, such a funny shape, full of toes and muscular curves. You stretch out your arms. An old woman's arms are ugly, I hate them. I wish I could stretch and see those slim arms turned gold by this sun, rising once again from their cotton sleeves. I hate mirrors, I hate what my face has become, full of gray and blue, in the shadow of wrinkles. It's a mineral face, as if it's been dotted with spots of rust, and cold as marble. The glorious features have been erased. It's nearly over for the face, for the living matter that we twist to make a grimace, or hold out for a kiss, or crease to express our rage. Soon they'll all be inert, those arms and legs, and that body, already flaccid and hard at the same time.

To curl up in a deep hole or be scattered to the four winds, I have not yet made my choice. I'm merely thinking about it and yet, I really don't have a clue. What I would like would be a rebirth, without pain, without bitterness, almost without a memory of what I was before. Perhaps I'd have a new House to cherish, and new brothers and sisters with whom I could run around in the silken grass. I'd let myself drift in the placid drowsiness of a siesta in the sun. Once again I'd feel the water, a touch too cold, running over my hands as I washed them before dinner. I'd pierce the tender flesh of a vegetable with my fork, and my tongue, like a shallow bed, would greet a stream of flavors. On rainy days I'd trace the rain drops on the glass with my fingertip. I'd put on freshly-washed clothes, and feel them rubbing softly against my young skin, smelling of laundry soap; again and again.

Perhaps I'd rather be reborn as a bear, or a fox, something that lives in the forest, and knows only its woods. Then all my life I'd wander along timeless paths through the trees, which would lead me, without my really knowing quite how, to the languid flow of a full river. There I would bend down to taste the mountain water from a clear spring rippling in the sun. I'd trust my vigorous paws to sink into the cool grass, trust the ways of the world, and remain perfectly ignorant of the end of things.

Entering this care home was a violent, implacable confrontation with my own disappearance. In itself, it did not come as a surprise; all our life we know that we have to die, and yet nothing ever prepares us for it, not even the death of others. When your body becomes weak, you are suddenly burdened with an accumulation of regrets that is so heavy, so unwieldy that they make the end of life unbearably sad. The joy in my heart has difficulty reviving, igniting.

I don't think when I was still at the House that I was completely despondent. I still felt a bit useful, I lived in a place where I had once flourished; I lived in the illusion that I would continue to be who I'd always been. I hadn't yet understood that all the little things we accumulate in a lifetime—our little passions, our little infatuations, favorite colors, books we'd read, ways to repot plants, the secret of a successful jam—all of that would disappear. And with me, everything Petite Mère and Petit Père had taught me, all the minor events that went to make up my character and who I was to others. The way Klaus, at the dinner table, took the time to serve water to us, his little sisters: that taught me how to be altruistic; the way I'd switch off the light, in the evening when Harriett asked me to: that taught me how to live with others; knowing when to let Louisa do her drawings in her room taught me to respect other people's private worlds.

As I got older, as if to slow the time being lost, unconsciously, as if to cling to the passage of the hours and stretch them out, or, quite simply, to prove to myself that my life had not been in vain, I began cultivating new skills. I searched within to find new resources, hidden faculties, that were mine alone: like children at school being urged to explore everything in order to find their passion, I experimented with various occupations—knitting, woodcutting, embroidery, writing, drawing. Through my fifties, I tried all sorts of things that I'd never deemed worthwhile before. Repairing things myself, playing the piano, standing at the window to imitate the song of the birds in the trees. I wasn't good at everything, and would quickly give up on some things, but this hunger for activity convinced me that I was still a work in progress, that I was still a soil where new essences could grow.

In my young old age I got the idea of taking over Petite Mère's studio on the veranda. I hadn't touched a thing since her death, or very little. The paintbrushes were still head to tail in their jars. Her last, unfinished canvases, bouquets of flowers painted with a rare violence, were crammed together facing the wall, as if ashamed of the sorrow with which they were saturated. My mother's neuralgia was there in its entirety, still vibrant forty years on, in the glare of the reds and the very abandonment with which the canvases were gathering dust. I cleaned the easel, and the brushes, but as the palettes were too damaged, I threw them out, still full of dried paint. They contained Petite Mère's innovative mixtures, the beautiful purples that she'd excelled at, now dry for forty years. I ran my finger over the shining rough surface of frozen mixtures, over the eternal colors. I could feel the streaks of the brush she had dipped into the pigment; hardened streaks, dead streaks. Phantom brushes strokes prolonged my hand. I resembled the person my mother would have been at the age of sixty.

The House was so lovely, in the hollow of blue garden. I wanted to capture it forever, in an image, the frank yellow of the sun on the white wooden boards, the blue reflected in the windows. I wanted to grasp the golden sequins that slid along the branches of the apple trees in the orchard. I came up with a project, initially rather vague, then obsessive. I would paint the House. I told myself—and this was my mistake—that I didn't need to know how to paint, since I had such a clear vision of what I wanted to project onto the canvas. I thought I would see the colors so precisely that nothing could come between me and the image of the House that I had in mind.

Petite Mère's tubes of paint were completely dry. I went down to the village and from the grocery store I ordered a canvas, just one, and an entire assortment of acrylics. The week I spent waiting for my order seemed endless. I was as restless as a child, so eager to start this project that had suddenly become crucial, even ineluctable.

No sooner had the mail carrier stopped his van by the letterbox than I had leapt down the steps at the front door to tear the package from his hands; I remember saying a hasty goodbye then rushing into the kitchen. There I tore the brown paper wrapping from the tubes of paint. I ran my hand over the rough off-white surface of the blank canvas, where I could picture very clearly how the House would stand out—it would be perfect, faithful, brilliant. I knew where I would hang the picture once it was finished and dry, all of which, I supposed, would take up the better part of a day; it would go straight onto the wall in the bedroom, so that Harriett would see it, too, when she settled silently on the cold sheets.

My hands were trembling with excitement and haste; I imagined the rich, sensual experience to come, fluid, with lines both full and sharp, and paint brushes that would behave, and do my bidding. I thought of Petite Mère, when she was painting, how she did it so easily, effortlessly, how she blurred the petals and, with an agile sweep of the brush, gave a velvet sheen to the corollas.

I took the easel out on the warm grass bathed in a fresh midday sun, and I propped it firmly on the ground. I stood facing the canvas, everything was ready, the palette pressing on my arm. The cream surface of the vertical rectangle seemed promising, with the tall façade of the House in the background on the orchard side, shining in a laughing splash of daylight.

Six hours later I collapsed in tears in the cold grass of late afternoon.

I threw out the hideous canvas, where horrid mixtures of colors had crusted, a monochrome of dirty browns, a color chart of mud and wet silt, the entire shore of the murky pond stirred up, from that cursed lake to deep in our guts. I sobbed with rage, my disappointment was huge, my inability to capture the House in the way I loved it, and everything it represented. The lines were all wrong, the perspective was vanishing, the windows childish; I had ruined the façade, the egg white color had been spoiled by a brown shadow I wanted to add at the last minute. At no point had my eyes been able to transmit to my hand the pure and joyful image of that House as I perceived it, full of our presence, and Harriett's, full of memories so beautiful that every instant of the day they wrenched my heart out, memories painful and contaminated with regret, grief, and old age encircling me like evil ivy.

I could take no more—the solitude, the wet grass, the unbearable absence of my family, both living and dead; I could take no more, suddenly, there on my knees in the cold shadow of the House, on that black earth that was staining my dress, staining my hands and my ankles. It all came out, in great, hiccupping, suffocating sobs, everything that was dispiriting about loving and living in a House that gives nothing in return, that does not help you to remember, that in spite of all your efforts allows itself to decay. Every winter, roof tiles fell, and it was worse during the summer storms, when entire trees came down in the forest, struck at random by the terrible arrows of light that shot from the clouds. I'd had repair work done, one job after another, year after year, yet the roof was falling to bits, and people told me the structure was rotting. I figured, well, it's beyond repair, the House is rotting and I'll rot along with it.

I imagined dying in my little bed, in a room strangled by creepers, covered with blue moss glowing faintly in a night as dark as a cave, with copper grass snakes curled up on the parquet floor. Reeds would pierce the floor and brown water would suddenly flood the room; I would become Petit Père and Uncle Bertie's nightmarish drowned woman, the gorgon strangled by seaweed.

I told myself that my end, and that of the House, would coincide, and then one fine day my ghost would awaken quite naturally, with Harriett's ghost in the next bed, suddenly visible to me, breathing deeply beneath the sheets. I would be the happiest person on earth, I would take her in my translucent arms, because among ghosts that is allowed, we see one another and we touch one another, I'm sure of it. We would go and build transparent cabins while the House was collapsing, and we'd continue to play in the ruins of worm-eaten wood. She'd say, You know, Isa, I looked everywhere for my sock, and I would tell her, Little critter, run up to the room, it's under your bed, stuck in the skirting board.

I won't die in the House, now. It's over. I won't find Harriett ever again, will I? I'm so afraid I'll die in this room in this old people's home, alone in my armchair, and that my ghost will be trapped in it. I'll see my body being taken away by the methodical nurses. Harriett will weep, waiting for me, she'll wonder where I am, why I haven't joined her, now that I'm dead. I've abandoned the House, the way I abandoned Harriett, the way I abandoned the only desire in my life, to live and die in my House. That was my struggle, which I decided on in childhood, when I sat reading on the window ledge; that was my secret glory, my kingdom to defend. I failed, I'm here, far away from the House, in a dreary room with a view on a parking lot. I'm old and yet I don't die. I left the House, and at the last minute I failed to play my role of the vestal who maintains the hearth. I failed, from every point of view. I haven't spoken to Klaus or Louisa in three years. I don't know where they are. I've lost the living.

Now I remember why I left. Why, this spring, I sold everything, gave everything away, closed the door, shuttered the windows. I left this spring, long after the botched painting, long after the terrible pain in my chest. Long after, even, my first fall down the stairs, my beloved spiral staircase, almost a member of the family: suddenly it was after my blood, flinging me down like a bad-tempered horse twisting and jerking under the saddle. I left. I left because the House was trying to kill me.

Greatly ashamed, I had to ask the village for help with cooking, with hanging out the sheets, with lighting the fire in the fireplace. I would look askance at whoever they sent me, because it was costing me a fortune and it was an intrusion, having this unwanted person in my solitude, messing about in my kitchen.

I watched with terror as the end of the House approached. I wept every night in my little bed, which was no longer that of a child, but of an old maid, an old orphan. I could no longer drag the logs to the hearth, and my room was cold, cold, like the salon, like the kitchen, like the damned bathroom with its green tiles. The wind came howling into the rooms, it crashed its way through the windows, fragile from years of rain and ice. The wood had rotted, rotted to the very marrow of the House, and I had rotted along with it.

This spring, when I left, the garden was more luxuriant than ever before. Plants, herbs, flowers, all had grown with unbelievable vitality, almost overnight, in a display of green that was as glaringly luminous as that of a poisonous jungle. All that greenery was suffocating, it seemed to emerge just when I was feeling everything was giving way inside me. The garden seemed to relish the prospect of my decrepitude, which had begun in the white wooden building that was repainted every year, so long ago, with the family. Ever since my fall in the staircase, which broke a few ribs and kept me stuck in bed—doctor's orders—my lungs had been wheezing with every intake of breath. The air—saturated with chlorophyll, heavy with pollen, powdered with bumblebees and honey bees—clogged my breathing, coating the back of my throat and drying my eyes. The flowers were not tended, the garden was left to run wild, the trees were heavy with beautiful, firm, round fruit, with skin oozing juice, fruit more radiant than ever. I awoke with my mind wandering, then opened the shutters: the garden bursting with sunlight was buzzing even more, and huge flies were banging brazenly against the windowpane.

For the first time, I felt overwhelmed by the House. My spot at the geriatric institution, reserved the previous autumn, in anticipation, was waiting for me, some thirty kilometers from the House. I told myself I really ought to stop everything, now, right away, because this summer there would be too many peaches in the orchard, groaning under the weight of their velvety down skin. With a great deal of resignation, and infinitely saddened, as I drank my tea in the kitchen, leaning against the sink, I told myself that everything here had become too painful. The House was shaky, I was on my knees, there was nothing left for us to do here, in this poisonous garden with its too-gorgeous fruit.

I left one morning in April, in a van driven by the village carpenter. In that van taking me to the institution were my armchair, my photo albums, a trunk full of clothes, a few books, and a box with Jésabel's letters. Deep in my pocket I had hidden a second set of keys to the House. For the duration of the trip I held them tight in my fist, so tight they hurt my skin with their metallic bite. I want to be buried with those keys. To be able to go home again when I'm dead.

I hardly remember that morning of moving. I was in a dreadful state of exhaustion and anger, distraught by the sacrifice of my life for that place, yet horribly sad to be leaving it, with an indescribable terror at what awaited. In that cool morning a fine rain was creating a sort of lavender foam, which softened the edge of the woods. I'd just taken my last shower in the bathroom with the green tiles. I went out through the porch, closed the door; my feet crunched on the gravel and every step weighed like a cloak of sandstone. My shoulders sank to the earth. The carpenter supported me out to the truck, because I couldn't see through my tears. At the very last moment, I no longer wanted to go, I cried out in a last desperate convulsion, it suddenly seemed unthinkable to leave our room, never again to see the stairway, the hall the kitchen, the salon with its hearth blackened by the flares of fire in our childhood, the veranda where Petite Mère is painting, humming, the floors above where my cousins run with quick little steps when we play, Louisa is brushing Harriett's hair in her well-lit room, Klaus is lumbering down from the attic like a bear, all of us are pushing and shoving in the corridor, he pinches my ribs, we have the same eyes, the same nose, he's my beloved older brother. What are Klaus and Louisa doing, while I'm fighting with myself on the threshold of the House? Why am I the only one on the battlefield, when the bugle is sounding, and the incredible violence of our shared ghosts is falling upon me? What is Harriett doing? It's an easy thing, to die, to leave everything for others to deal with, the memories and the furniture, the toy chests no one can empty because they're still full of everything that no longer exists. All I feel is anger, the anger I had on leaving the House, the anger I still have as I see everything again, imagining the House still collapsing, without me, the garden gorging itself on the putrefaction of the dead as they are entangled in the roots, swallowed by the lake. The façade receded in the rearview mirror, narrow, pointed at the pale sky, with all its windows empty.

I have never cried as much as that morning when I left the House. On entering the geriatric institution I lived through every time of mourning at once. Everything landed on me—Petit Père, Petite Mère, Great-Aunt Babel, Harriett—then Harriett for a second time, as if I were being told, once again, that she was no more, that I would never hear her voice again, that she would never come at Christmas, that I would have to get used to having nothing of her beyond faded photographs and memories. The roof where the rain is falling, the murmurs I share with Harriett, before we fall asleep to the grownups' comforting mumblings as they clear the table downstairs, the blue room of a night without fear, without ghosts.

They are a terrible thing, an old woman's tears, everyone

knows they are inconsolable. The sorrows run too deep, are too vital, they have become a part of one's self. My sorrows and my anger are all I have left.

I'm thirsty.

I'll send for the nurse, in a little while. I'll ask her to find the phone number for Klaus Aberfletch and Louisa Aberfletch-Saggiatini. And then I'll call them, for the first time in years, and we'll talk about the white House among the blue fir trees, and the games we played on every floor, and the parquet that creaked to the sound of our laughter, and the branches heavy with sap that stuck to our hands.

Maybe together we'll win the last battle of our precious wars, Klaus, Louisa, and I. With each throw of the spear, pierce the silence; brandish a shield, the three of us. And as a family, level the rubble at last. Our little sister would smile from behind the windowpane, all alone and transparent in the big cold House.